Snaketrack

"Reckon a man could find some work? I ain't proud. I plowed a field for winter rye once. But I rope a lot better than I plow."

"How are you with a gun? And at drinking by yourself?"

"Explain yourself, mister."

"I've got some range lined up, a basin called Snaketrack. It's a private lease, but there's no way of knowing how the man's going to feel who's been leasing it up till now. Knowing him, I figure it's a good idea to be hiring men for their guns as well as their ropes."

"Another good idea might be to find another range."

"There's nothing else to lease. I'll pay thirty a month and found. More when I can. If things get too rough, I won't hold it against you for quitting."

"Maybe you wouldn't, but I would. If I can have a month in advance, I'd be obliged . . ."

FRANK BONHAM
Snaketrack

AVON BOOKS NEW YORK

AVON BOOKS
A division of
The Hearst Corporation
105 Madison Avenue
New York, New York 10016

First Avon Books Printing: September 1989

AVON TRADEMARK REG. U.S. PAT. OFF. AND IN OTHER COUNTRIES, MARCA
REGISTRADA. HECHO EN U.S.A.

Printed in the U.S.A.

K–R   10   9   8   7   6   5   4   3   2   1

For
My Mother and Father
With Affection

—1—

CARMODY LAY ON the bunk, smoking a Mexican cigar and watching shadows move over the ceiling of the caboose. As a crash of couplings reverberated down the slowing train, he glanced through a window into the twilight of a broad wash. At once he recognized a familiar outline of mesas and plum-blue mountains, and he swung his legs over the side of the bunk and stood up. He stretched, yawning loudly. Then he flexed his shoulders vigorously, shaking off the last of his sleep. All afternoon he had slept, while the cattle-train smoked northward over the plains toward a range of mountains.

It was drafty in the caboose. He could smell rain and coal-smoke, and the heavy scent of cattle. The rain-smell was fragrant. Even the odor of the cattle pleased him. Cattle were no different from anything else a man owned, he reflected: a man's own cattle always smelled good to him.

He began looking for his things. He was a tall man in his middle twenties, big-boned but without any extra flesh, and there was a hard-shouldered look to him. Carmody's face was good-humored, yet with bluntness in the mouth and chin. He wore a four-day beard of the same chestnut color as his cigar. His hair was roached like the mane of a mule.

From the weary trash of the caboose, he assembled his belongings—a blanket roll, a booted rifle, some paper parcels. He piled them on the bunk. Then, walking to the rear, he opened the door to a roar of cold mountain wind laced with coal-smoke. He stepped out into the rush and clatter of the platform and looked down upon the wide canyon of the Soledad River, brimming with dusk. A little green was left in the bottom, but the slopes were brown and dead. A village ahead, huddled against the foot of a mesa, was sprinkled with a few early lights.

It was a melancholy time of year to be coming home; a melancholy time of day. Carmody flipped the cigar away and briskly went back into the car.

A man in a cowpuncher's bleached denim trousers and a black horsehide jacket had come down the ladder from the cupola. He stood in the shimmering warmth of the stove, rubbing his hands together. He was slim and wiry, with the whittled hips of a horseman. His face and hands were red with cold.

"This it?" he asked. "Looks like the end of everything."

"This is it," Carmody told him. The puncher's name was Creed Davis. Carmody had hired him to help feed and water his newly-purchased cattle on the trip from El Paso to this rugged northeast corner of New Mexico. At Soledad, he would take his pay and ride a day-coach back.

"You ranch near here, eh?" Creed asked.

". . . Used to," Carmody said. "I've got a little land on Crooked River. Good grazing country, when you can find it under the snow. Ten months of winter, and two months that you couldn't call summer."

"It don't look so bad," Creed contended.

"Wait till it starts snowing! We're feeding the cattle straw out of our pants-cuffs by spring."

"Reckon a man could find work this time of year?"

"There may be a few ranches hiring."

Carmody had anticipated the question. The easy, and obvious, answer was that winter was layoff time in the high country. But he had taken a liking to Davis. He was a springy little man who had not rested all the way from the border. Carmody preferred to give him this answer, which left the gate open.

Creed finished collecting his cowpuncher's-gather and rolled a cigarette. "You coming back to ranch, fella," he asked, "or are you selling these cows?"

"I'm back to ranch," Carmody told him.

"Reckon you're all fixed for hands, eh?"

"No." Carmody smiled as he shook his head.

Suddenly Creed threw the match into the coal-box. "Damn it!" he said. "I don't happen to have one of my cards, but I punch cows, and I haven't worked for three months. That's what I've been getting at. What did you think I meant?"

"I thought you wanted a job," Carmody said, and when Creed's angry frown remained he added, "but not necessarily the kind I could give you."

"I ain't proud," Creed frowned. "I plowed a field for winter rye, once. But I rope better than I plow."

"How are you with a gun? And at drinking by yourself?"

Staring at Carmody, Creed snapped a match in his fingers. "I expect there's a train out of Soledad in the morning, ain't there?"

"Sure," Carmody said casually. "Likely there'll be some cattle going out. Maybe you can take another bunch back down."

Creed walked to the door and opened it. But he turned to say roughly, "If you've used me to help move any wet cattle, Carmody, I'll break that rifle over your head."

"They're all mine," Carmody smiled. "They don't fight over cattle in this country, anyhow—they fight over land. Hard enough to feed the cattle you already have, without stealing any more. I've got land, you understand, but not enough for the cattle I own, and what I'm bringing in."

"If I'd got past sixth grade, maybe I could savvy mathematics like that."

"I've some range lined up," Carmody explained. "You see, there's one big outfit up here, and a handful of little fellows. There's a little private land leased and some on the Jicarilla reservation. This is a private lease I'm looking at, the biggest one of all, but there's no way of knowing how the man's going to feel who's been leasing it up to now. Knowing him, I reckon a good idea might be to hire men for their guns as well as their ropes."

3

"Another good idea might be to lease something else," Creed suggested.

"There's nothing else to lease. I've more or less made arrangements for this piece of land. I'll begin stocking it with the cows we've brought up."

The train was jolting to a stop. Thick animal odors crowded in from the stock-pens. There was a thudding of restless hoofs, a man's voice shouting something. A lantern swung in a red arc past the window.

Carmody's eyes judged the cowpuncher. It was a sharp testing of what was behind his face besides the dry good humor he had grown accustomed to. Creed stood truculently under the inspection. He was shorter than Carmody. He had shallow blue eyes and a large mouth, a rude energy that kept some part of his body always in motion, and he wore his Stetson on the side of his head, as if he did not want men to think he was any smaller than he was.

After a long instant, Carmody said, "I'll pay thirty a month and found. More when I can. If things get too rough, I wouldn't hold it against you for quitting."

Creed balanced his blanket roll on his shoulder. "Maybe you wouldn't, Carmody, but I would. . . . If I can have the first month in advance," he said, "I'd be obliged."

With a last, shuddering yank, the train came to rest. In the caboose, the silence ached. The lamp swung gently with chucklings of coal oil. Carmody put a hand on Creed's shoulder.

"You know, you're a lot bigger than you look, Creed. Maybe as big as the job. Well, let's go see how many cows I've got left. . . ."

While the cars were kicked onto the siding, they stood in the dead weeds beside the tracks. On a cold wind, night overflowed the broken eaves of the mesa looking above the town. Continents of dark clouds collided in the sky; the air was musty with rain. Creed buttoned his jacket.

Carmody was watching two men striding down the line of cattle cars. They ducked under the loading ramp and came on. The pens rocked with cattle bawling against confinement, locomotives, and the weather. Carmody's hands slowly squeezed shut. Recognizing the pair, he was breathless and ready.

Momentarily he let his eyes move on—past a line of wintry poplars, across an uptilted vista of shacks, privies, leafless family-orchards, and picket fences, on into the town. More lights were coming on and evening smoke gathered in the heavy air. It had been a year since he had left Soledad; he found himself impatient to see what things had changed, what things were the same. His glance came back. There was a sharp and swift restlessness in him, a nettling of his whole being.

Creed glanced at him and saw the hard shine of his eyes. "I hope I ain't going to start earning that pay before I get a cup of Arbuckle in me," he drawled. "Who are they?"

"An old employer and his ramrod," Carmody said. "Remind me to tip my hat."

The shadow of Carmody's Stetson hung before his face. The taller of the men, very spare and with a hard-fleshed look, stopped and scratched a match against the caboose. Relighting a half-smoked cigar, he dropped the match and let it burn out on the grade.

"You men with these cattle?" he asked.

"They're with us," Carmody said. He watched the man, wondering when recognition would come to him.

"I'm clearing a pen for you," Holt Bannerman declared. "You'll have to move them out. I want my animals in the cars before the storm breaks."

Carmody inspected the sky. "Smells like it's already rained some."

"It rained this afternoon. Snow before Thanksgiving, I reckon. Another early winter." He began pulling on a rawhide glove. "My foreman will help you get your cattle onto the community pasture, yonder on the mesa. Good night."

"You figure my Shorthorns will stand the weather better than your Herefords?" Carmody asked.

The rancher had already turned. He halted and swung back, and taking the cigar out of his mouth he came doggedly to where the man stood in the weeds.

5

Frank Bonham

"Your cattle have had their trip. They'll bed down soon enough. I want the buck and pitch out of mine before morning."

Carmody said nothing. Suddenly Bannerman's hand brought his cigar down. He stepped close. He stared into Carmody's face for a moment and all at once caught his breath.

"Carmody!" he said. "By God, you had your guts, coming back!"

"You always said I did," Carmody observed.

The dullness of Bannerman's surprise gave way. Carmody saw a surge of anger mount through his face, his eyes standing out smudged and bitter and dark. Bannerman seized his arm. "Where is she? Damn you, Carmody, where is Ruth?"

Carmody glanced down at the corded hand holding his arm. He put his gaze on the rancher's face. "If I knew, you wouldn't get it out of me that way."

After a moment Bannerman dropped his hand, but he remained close, savagely dominating. He had the close grain of oak and a strenuous energy of mind and body. Carmody had known him as employer and almost as father-in-law. He had learned from him that it was possible to respect a man and still despise him.

"Where is she?" Bannerman repeated. "Where did you leave her? In some pigsty in El Paso?"

Bannerman's foreman hastily pushed between them as Carmody's shoulders stirred, his face darkening with a quick flare of anger. Morgan Wiley put his back to Tom Carmody and said, "Easy now! Mr. Bannerman, let's settle this about cattle first. Let's find the owner of these critters."

"You've found him," Carmody stated.

Bannerman looked back at the dark, lowing cars. "Your whole ranch wouldn't buy fifty Shorthorns like those," he grunted.

"No," Carmody agreed. "It sure wouldn't."

The locomotive bleated. Above this sound tumbled a far-off cannonading of thunder. Wiley inspected Carmody carefully.

6

"Buy them with dollars, or *pesos?*" he inquired, with a sly grin. He was a robust, sauntering man with crisp sideburns and a truculent mouth. His hair was thick and curly, growing low on his neck.

Carmody remembered a *cantina* across the river from El Paso, and the kind of company he had been in when Wiley, down to buy supplies for Bannerman's big Cross Anchor ranch, had run across him six months ago. . . .

"With Durham tags," he said.

"You must have done all right in the Mexican army."

Carmody spotted the ramrod's gambit—to draw the subject as far from Ruth Bannerman as possible. Morgan Wiley knew what every man on Bannerman's payroll learned sooner or later—that the quickest way to fury or favor was through Ruth. And there was suddenly fury in the air tonight.

"Who said I was in the Mexican army?" Carmody asked him.

"There was enough braid on that Spik you were drinking with to decorate a Christmas tree," Wiley declared.

Bannerman was watching him with less heat now, but with carefulness and suspicion. His anger was still there, but he was plainly puzzled. After a moment he said, "I'd like five minutes with you alone." He put his foot on the step of the caboose and mounted to the platform.

Carmody looked at Creed Davis. "Why don't you hike up to the Great Western and get us a room? You might park this gear of mine up, too."

Creed regarded Bannerman with cool inspection. "Sure you don't want me to wait?"

Carmody winked, "Sure," and swung up the ladder.

Inside, there was the dim yellow light of the lamp and the dry heat of the stove. Bannerman bit the tip off a fresh cigar and held the end against the rosy heat-stove until it smoked.

He asked suddenly, "Where's Ruth?"

"Did somebody say I knew?"

"You've been away a year. I figured you'd met her somewhere."

"Is that why you sent Wiley coyoting after me to El

7

Paso? I haven't seen her since you took her home from my place that night. Don't blame me if you couldn't hold her."

"She came home to me—remember that," Bannerman snapped. "*You* couldn't keep her—the sowbelly bridegroom for the cornpone bride!"

The phrase had humiliated once. It angered now, but not as it had angered when it was true. Carmody asked, drily, "What is it that makes Ruth too good for the kind of man you used to be yourself?"

Bannerman for an instant looked blank, as if surprised by an idea which had never occurred to him. But then he gave a short laugh. "God forbid I should ever have been your kind of man! Pussyfooting around, making love to the boss's daughter! Quitting a good job to starve on ten sections of sage and rock! You had a good thing on Cross Anchor, Carmody. You were learning how to ranch—and getting paid for it."

Carmody nodded, soberly but with a glint of humor. "Sure—I learned how to measure the thickness of potato peelings outside the cook-shack, and not to hire one-armed wranglers, because they were apt to get hurt and be on the boss's hands. But I never did learn how to fall in love with a girl without her finding out about it."

"She found out," Bannerman said, "but thank God she had the good sense not to fall in love with you!"

"I had an idea she did," Carmody said. "But she'd had her mind made up by you for so long that she was afraid to make up her own."

Bannerman blew smoke at the lamp and unexpectedly smiled. "And you claim you knew Ruth! Carmody, nobody ever made up Ruth's mind about anything. If she hadn't been willing to come back with me that night, I could never in God's world have made her."

"But three days later," Tom pointed out, "she ran off again."

Bannerman frowned, reflectively. "Did you ever have any idea what I wanted for Ruth?"

"I figured you wanted her to have everything you thought she ought to have. Including a cattle king for a husband.

And some little cattle princes. And a ranch she could tie in with yours some day, when you'd gone to glory."

"I wanted her to have everything she needed to make her happy. Whether it was a man or a hundred thousand acres of grassland. But I wanted her to learn the difference between a whim and a need. So she didn't always get what she wanted while she was growing up. I never did one thing for Ruth without a reason," he said. "I didn't make the gift of a horse or withhold the gift of a gown, without a reason."

"And after she was a big girl she knew her own mind, just like you planned. But the first thing she didn't want was you," Carmody laughed softly.

Bannerman took the cigar from his mouth, anger whipping darkly into his face. With the cigar palmed, the smoke fumed upward through his fingers—a small gesture, yet remembered well, and somehow a key to arrogance—the mannerism of a man whose cattle covered more hills than any cattleman in a week's ride, a man who expected and liked to be watched.

"A week after you left," he said, "I started for your place with a rifle across my saddle. I don't know now why I turned back."

"I don't either. I was waiting."

"If you've come back for a blow-off," Bannerman said with a bite, "you don't have to hunt all over New Mexico for it."

Carmody settled his boots carefully on the floor. There was the width of the car between them. The light glinted dully on the backstrap of his Colt as he moved. He seemed to space his words carefully.

"I'm not back for a blow-off. I'm back to ranch. What's happened is finished, as far as I'm concerned. What's going to happen will depend on you."

"What do you mean?"

"I mean I need land. I'll get it—legally. But I won't be pushed by anybody who thinks he ought to have it instead of me. I know where I'm going this time."

Bannerman's face was suddenly watchful. He took the cigar in his teeth. He said, "If you put those cattle on any land of mine, I can tell you damn quick where you're going." He walked to the platform of the car. He turned back, his face set. "Get your cattle out. I'll furnish hands to hold them till you decide what you're going to do."

Carmody merely smiled and moved through the door, but as he passed, the rancher seized his arm. "By God, don't try to take anything else of mine! I haven't changed."

"I expect I have," Carmody said. "I wouldn't give a girl up this time—not if I wanted her. I don't think I want Ruth. But if I find I do, and she comes back, it won't be you that keeps me away from her."

Bannerman said, "Let's see if you'll back that up when it happens."

He dropped to the grade and strode away toward the station.

—2—

A SHORT DISTANCE down the crowded aisle between the cars and the pens, Morgan Wiley waited with his coat collar turned up. Carmody heard Bannerman say something to him as he passed, and saw Wiley's brief nod. When Carmody came up, the ramrod stepped out so that Tom had to stop.

"The old man is sore," he commented wryly.

"What about me?" Carmody asked. "Don't I look sore?"

"Ever since you stepped out of that caboose," said Wiley, "you've looked like a guy holding four aces in a blue-chip game."

Carmody started by him, smiling, but he did not move out of the way. "Tom," he said, his eyes steady and dark, wideset under thick brows.

Carmody sighed. "Get to it. Ask me where she is."

"Where is she?"

"I don't know."

"Like hell you don't."

"You ought to know. You sneaked around after me for a week in El Paso and Juarez. My shadow even got to clearing its throat like you."

Wiley's hand closed on Carmody's forearm. His face, unshaven, pinched with cold, was bare of humor. He was angrily intent on something which had been in his mind for a long time.

"Don't give me that, Tom," he snapped. "You've been

11

with Ruth! You've parked her some place. And you're going back to her.''

"Why don't you wait around, then? Maybe I'll let you be best man.''

"Is she waiting for you?" Wiley insisted. "By God, I'm going to know!''

"You're going to know a little bit more about Tom Carmody, too, if you don't let go my arm.''

Wiley's hand fell away. Staring at Carmody, he seemed trying to make up his mind to something. Then he said, frowning at a button of Tom's jacket, "You didn't know this. Ruth and me were engaged once, Tom, before she ever looked at you. *That's* where I come into this.''

Carmody shrugged. "I know. Ruth told me. What's it got to do with me?''

Wiley's anger surged to the surface.

"I'm going to tell you something," he stated, "and don't you ever forget it. If you've been living with Ruth, I'll kill you. If you're hiding where she is, I'll whip you so you'll scare your own pony when he sees you.''

He stepped aside. Carmody chewed on his cigar for a moment. Then he said, "You didn't ask if Ruth and I are married. Ask me sometime. I might answer a straight question like that." He walked on.

Ahead, he saw Bannerman leaving the adobe station building. He reached the plank shore surrounding it. On a baggage truck sat four cowpunchers—silent, sombrero'd men in bullhide chaps and thick jackets. One of the men spoke to him.

"Howdy, Tom!" It was the bull-voice of big Jim Shaniko, range foreman on Cross Anchor since Tom's firing.

"Hello, Jim," Tom said. "Early winter, eh?''

"Cold snap," Shaniko said. "Warm up ag'in. Who's going to spend the night here—us or you?''

"I'm satisfied with things as they are. Why don't you go uptown and get some chuck?''

"Why don't you let us by moving your cattle out?''

"And break those critters' legs?" Tom said. "See you later.''

As he made the double row of trees at the foot of town,

he heard the first pelting bullets of the rain against his hat-brim. He hurried to the sidewalk, and the storm suddenly swept over the rimrock and assaulted the dry leaves, the wooden awnings, the flat, and the roofs of Soledad. Women screeched at children, horses chopped briskly along, and turnouts rattled by. Fall snapped in the air.

Almost surprised, Carmody thought: *I'm glad I came back!* He was glad all through. It was home range, where he had had his boyhood enjoyments and hurts, where he had worn the prestige of being a Cross Anchor cowboy and the patches of Cross Anchor pay, and now suddenly he was about to be part of it again.

He saw the wet backs of ponies gleaming at racks. This chill autumn's end, cattle were being trailed from mountainous summer pastures to the mesas; beef cattle would keep the shipping pens filled for a month. He passed a saloon and walked under leaking awnings toward the law office of Judge Myron Cincinnatus, stopping before the door of a tin-roofed outside stairway. The bank and a mercantile occupied the lower floor of a two-story building. Upstairs were the office and town quarters of Judge Cincinnatus, who augmented a lawyer's income as Indian agent to the Jicarilla Apaches.

Just before he reached the top of the stairs, a door opened and a fan of light glowed on the landing. A girl stood in the doorway. Carmody stood motionless. Then he said banteringly: "Hello, Papoose!"

Laura Cincinnatus stood very still. Her hand went up to touch the porcelain knob. Then she took a breath and said, "There's only one man I know with the bad manners to call me 'Papoose.' But he's a Mexican general now, so you can't be the same."

"It's General Carmody, back from the tortilla revolution," Carmody said.

He could not see enough of her face to make out what she was thinking, but he heard her say, with a soft gladness, "Tom Carmody . . . !" and then she stopped. "Are you alone, Tom?"

"Just me, and a puncher I parked somewhere. No woman, despite what you might have heard."

He went into the small parlor with its plastered adobe walls and deep windows. Red Indian rugs patterned the floor. The softness of them under his feet made him feel like a treading cougar. Carmody watched the girl turn from the door. She was small and dark-haired in a light-gray gown snug about the hips and full below. She turned quickly with a smile, placing her palms against the door, a vivid gladness in her face.

"It—it's such a surprise, Tom. Everybody said you'd never come back."

"What did you say?"

"I made a bet with myself—I bet you'd be back. . . . Are you hungry?"

"I could eat my way through a steer."

As she arranged his jacket to dry on a chair near the corner fireplace, he saw the unbelievable slenderness of her waist and the sweet fullness of her breast, and he took a deep breath. White women and white women's cooking—you couldn't beat them.

In the kitchen, she slid a coffee pot onto the stove and began to slice a round loaf of bread. Carmody asked her where the judge was. "Out somewhere," she told him. "Collecting donations for his starving Indians, I expect. He'll be back soon."

"How is he?"

"Dad's fine. Still trimming his mustache like Chief Justice Waite, and writing legal opinions on everything under the sun. He had an opinion published in the *Inquirer* last week. But I doubt if it will come to the attention of the Supreme Court."

She went by him, carrying a steaming plate of mulligan. Tom took a seat at the table. "Some day," he sighed, "somebody's going to discover the judge's papoose has grown up, and the parlor is going to be full of cowpunchers with boiled collars and bunkhouse haircuts."

She gave him a quick, impudent glance. "Oh, I'm asked to a social once in a while." She took her seat, smiling.

"Who do you go with?" Carmody asked.

"Mike Ridge, mostly."

"No!" Carmody said, with a pained expression.

"Yes! He's only thirty-some, not old at all. He's as distinguished-looking as ever—and after all not every girl lands a town marshal."

"I didn't mean that. I meant . . ." The banter was out of his eyes. He frowned.

"You meant he didn't treat Pete Trinidad right," Laura said quietly. "But Pete would still be in prison for rustling if Mike hadn't got him out."

"He wouldn't have been in prison in the first place," Carmody said shortly, "if Ridge had investigated the evidence that jugged him. Taking the word of a fool like Jim Shaniko against a good Mexican like Pete! Everybody knew they'd been feuding over Rosa Cordray. Everybody but Ridge."

When he looked at her, he saw her eyes chilling. "Mike is a good friend of Dad's and mine, Tom. I happen to believe he's honest."

"I was in Mexico with a fellow who didn't. He left here because he couldn't get work. He couldn't get work because he'd been in prison for two years. He'd been in prison because Ridge put him there. I mean Trinidad. . . . What's all this tub-thumping for the good marshal?" he demanded. "You aren't going to marry him, are you? Do you want all your kids to be born with tin badges and Buffalo Bill mustaches?"

Laura put her hands on the table as if to rise, her eyes angry; but immediately Carmody relaxed.

"Excuse me, Papoose," he sighed. "I'll stay after school for that. I get a little hot when I think about Trinidad."

"I have the feeling that you get a little hot about lots of things. You've changed—do you know that?"

Carmody tore off half a slice of bread. "Everybody changes. You've changed yourself."

"But I hope I'm not as—as cocksure as you."

"What's the matter?" he grinned. "Have I been wearing my hat on the side of my head again?"

"You walked in here looking as though you owned the place."

"I learned something down there," Tom said. "If you

15

walk in as though you owned a place, sometimes you wind up owning it. I found out that if you're going to hit at all, you've got to hit first. The rebels didn't—and they got licked.''

Her expression was lofty. "The only thing better than hitting first is to be so clever you don't have to hit at all.''

He shrugged. "Well, I came back to ranch, Laura, not fight. I've got a trainload of Durhams with me. The best-looking cattle this country's ever seen.''

"Cattle like that cost a lot of money, don't they?''

"Practically a fortune.''

"Do you have a fortune?''

"I've got a receipt for the cattle. Is that what you mean?''

Her eyes remained troubled. "I suppose that's what I mean. You hadn't the money to hire a cowpuncher when you left, but you come back with a fortune in Shorthorn cattle.''

"And no sheriff on my trail," said Tom.

Laura shook her head. "I don't doubt you, Tom. But what will you do with them? You've got a couple of hundred cattle already, and hardly range for a hundred. What will you do with a hundred and fifty more?''

"I'll get range.''

"Where? There isn't a grazing lease in Union County of the size you'll need, except for the Tignal Jones ranch. And you know who leases *that* land!''

Her gaze remained intently on his face, a crease of wonder between her eyes, and now Tom's eyes came up teasingly. "I know who *has* leased it—up to now.''

Laura did not move. Her hands fell to her lap. "Tom Carmody! You aren't going to try to take Snaketrack from Holt Bannerman!''

Tom chuckled. "He doesn't own Snaketrack, Laura, just because he's leased it for twelve years. It's lease land. And the way I remember it, his lease is about up for renewal. What if Tig Jones leases to me this time?''

"*Has* he leased to you?''

Tom spoke with the edge of a smile.

"He wrote me last summer that I could have a five-year

16

lease, on terms to be arranged. Laura, those Shorthorns are only the first of twenty-five hundred head I'm going to put on Snaketrack. Bannerman's been as big as he's ever going to be. I'm just starting to grow.''

Laura stood up. She went to the window and looked out, and then turned angrily. "I wish Dad were here to hear this! . . . You mean that on the word of an old fool who hasn't been sober in fifteen years you've bought ten thousand dollars' worth of cattle! A man who put his own ranch in trust because even *he* didn't trust himself!''

"I know this much," Tom said. "Tig's always hated Bannerman. Bannerman kept chopping away at Snaketrack until Tig finally gave up and leased to him. Bannerman's stood over that land ever since, daring anybody to take it away from him.''

He saw that her fists were clenched, her cheeks flushed, and his awareness of her concern for him made important this test of his appearance in her eyes, sobered his look.

"Look, Laura. A man who fears to lose should never play. If he is afraid to shove in his blue chips on the strength of the hand dealt him, he will never make his stake, never get anywhere.''

Laura regarded him coolly.

"I've heard it said that a man studies his adversary as well as the cards he holds. Do you think for one minute that Bannerman will simply move off the land and let you have it? Is that what you're counting on?''

"I've got over counting on anything. If Bannerman wants to get heated up over it—that's up to him." Then, abruptly, he smiled. "It's not the end of the world, Papoose. Just Bannerman's world.''

She sat down to stir gritty sugar into her coffee. "Another of Bannerman's worlds came to an end a year ago, Tom. You ended that one, too.''

"No. I only helped a little.''

Laura did not look up. "What about Ruth, Tom? Did you meet her in El Paso, as they say?''

He had an obscure need to tell someone about himself and Ruth. He knew the furtive, grinning stories that must have gone around. He knew they must have come to

17

Laura's ears, too, and for some reason it was important to him that she should know the truth.

"No," he said. "I didn't meet her anywhere. We were through the night Bannerman took her out of my wagon and drove her home. In a way, he was the one who pushed us into it in the first place. We'd started going to dances, while I was still his range-boss. So he began ramping down on her. Well, it made us mad. We decided to get married on my ten sections, after Bannerman fired me."

Laura was listening without meeting his eyes. Tom frowned.

"So one night I met her at Indian Rock. We were getting into the wagon for the drive to the railroad when Bannerman came along in his cut-under buggy. He said, 'Ruth, get in here,' and she asked me, 'What'll I do, Tom?' I told her to make up her own mind. . . . You see, I figured—"

She looked quickly at him. "I think I know what you figured."

"She got out of my wagon and into the buggy," Tom said. "I was so mad that for a week I thought of going after him. I was mad about being called a sowbelly bridegroom. I made up my mind he'd lick my boots before I was through. But I knew I couldn't do much on ten sections, so I drove all my cows into the hills and took off."

"And now you're back" she said softly, ". . . to make him lick your boots."

"That's part of it. The rest is just that I know where I'm going—and nobody's going to stop me."

There was concern, almost sadness, in Laura's expression. "But the big part," she said, "is that you're going to break him, isn't it?"

The smile was out of his face. He looked soberly past her, at the dark sheen of the window, hearing the hiss of the rain. "I wouldn't be surprised," he said.

Tom helped her with the dishes, but when, at nine o'clock, the judge still had not come, he said:

"I'd like to put something in the safe. Can you open it?"

Laura started to carry a lamp into the office, but Tom stopped her. "I don't want to advertise that I've got anything to put in a safe. There ought to be enough light in there without a lamp."

"You're full of mysteries tonight," she told him. "I never will know half of what happened down there."

She opened the safe. Rain streamed from the wooden gutters outside the windows. He unfastened a money-belt under his shirt and installed it in the safe. Then he stood up, half a foot taller than she, a lean and looming man with a tired smile. "Let it be on my conscience, Laura. You're too young for worries."

"But it will be on my mind."

He donned his warm, damp jacket. As he stepped onto the landing, she followed. Suddenly her hand came from behind her. She held an envelope. She was smiling secretly.

"This came a month ago."

He looked at it. He had the kind of thrill one had on hearing a long-remembered voice in the next room. The handwriting was Ruth Bannerman's—it was addressed to him, in care of Judge Cincinnatus.

"I thought I ought to have a surprise for you, too," said Laura. "I see the postmark is Albuquerque. What do you suppose that means? That she's on her way home?"

Carmody pocketed the letter. "I'll take it up with my attorney," he said soberly. "When he comes in, tell him I'll be back in the morning."

—3—

CARMODY TOOK POSSESSION of the last room in the Great Western Hotel, a sort of kennel under an outside stairway. There was a blue graniteware washpan, a bucket of cold water, a baking-powder can full of soft soap. The blankets smelled of perspiration and dampness.

He procured a pitcher of hot water, and shaved. His jowls, burned darkly by the suns of Mexico, were brown as cordovan. He had scarcely faced himself in a mirror this past year. He looked for the brashness Laura had claimed to see in him. He recognized that his mouth was too wide and his nose thick through the bridge. His cheekbones were prominent. He would always look hungry, he thought, but if there was visible evidence of brashness it was in the set of his mouth. When he smiled, he lifted only one side of his mouth. It did something cynical to his eyes.

He started to buckle on his Colt, but hesitated. No, he thought, I'll be damned if I'll give him the satisfaction.

Then he remembered the letter from Ruth. He drew the rumpled envelope from his pocket. After a moment he took a match from a tin box beside the lamp. He held the two of them, the envelope and the match, and then he sighed, tossed the match back, and opened the letter.

It was like reading a dead man's mail, because the Tom Carmody who might have been excited by it had died a long time ago.

Tom dear: I hope that some hot-headed people I know have learned their lessons by now. I know I

have. Dad couldn't frighten me again. And I think
he must know it.

And you, Tom, should realize something, too—
that we lost each other that night because you wouldn't
help me stand up to him. You were bluffed out as
much as I.

I am in Albuquerque, on my way home. I hope I
shall find you still waiting, as you will find me,

Your own,
Ruth.

He dropped the letter in the airtight stove. He was
almost sorry he could not feel it more keenly, the death of
this love that had made such a change in his life.

When he went out, rain had filled the street-ruts with
dark, winding ribbons of water. In the mountains, thunder
growled. He thought of the crowded pens at the station.
Until the freight agent went home, there was the danger
that Bannerman might throw the fear into him and get him
to unlock the cars. Turning up the collar of his jacket, he
drifted down the street.

A man in overalls and a mackinaw came from the Great
Western Saloon as he passed it. He stood on the gleaming
boardwalk, moving his shoulders like a man feeling
packstraps and then, hearing Carmody's boots on the walk,
he turned and peered murkily at him. Carmody saw the
large, petulant face, and knew him.

"Hello, Chunk," he said. "How's my veal this season?"

"I don't eat your veal," Chunk McAllister said in
querulous ill-nature. He was a big, florid man with a
pocked face, discolored by whiskey, and a mind that had
been reasonably complicated until a logging accident had
scaled it down to childish proportions. He made a living
trapping coyotes and lobos for Bannerman. He could be
joshed just so far, Carmody recalled, less when he had
been drinking, and this was one of his bad nights.

"Who the hell are you?" Chunk demanded, and Carmody
moved so that the light coming through the frosted glass
doors struck him.

"Oh . . . Tom! . . . Been gone a spell, ain't you?" Chunk said.

Carmody said he had been away a while, and the other man looked at him with a vacancy in his eyes. He said abruptly, "Bunch of damn' cheapskates."

Carmody laughed. "Come on. I'll buy you a drink."

Chunk wiped his mouth and said, "Well, I—I wasn't thinkin' of that, Tom—" but he turned quickly and went through the double doors with him. He wore a stubble of whiskers with red, itchy patches under the chin.

The saloon was stifling with smells of wet woolen clothing and tobacco. Cowpunchers in muddy boots and damp coats packed the small, dirt-floored room. Along the left-hand wall ran a varnished bar with a barrel of beer on a mahogany trestle. A bartender was skimming suds with an ivory knife. So that there might be no loose talk about beer, Chunk said:

"I might just take a whiskey, Tom."

Tom bought whiskeys and turned to look over the room. It was noisy with overloud voices, pool balls clattering, chairs scraping. These men had been having their troubles with cattle and greasy trails, and some would go out at midnight to relieve other riders trying to keep herds bunched during the storm. They were taking on all the whiskey they could without running afoul of watchful foremen.

Carmody's eyes found Creed Davis. He was squeezed among a crowd of men around a table, but the table was hidden from view. Then he heard Holt Bannerman's loud laughter at the table where Creed stood. The rest of the cowboys began to laugh, and an old man's voice cried:

"That's fifty bucks, Bannerman—that's fifty bucks!"

Creed saw Carmody, then, and jerked his head. "Tom—look at this!"

Carmody went over to stand with him. Bannerman sat at a table with the old rancher, Tignal Jones, who owned the big Snaketrack iron. Morgan Wiley stood glumly behind his employer's chair, his dark hair tousled, disapproval in his face. In the middle of the table was a glass jug with a perforated piece of rawhide tied over the neck. On a carpet of earth at the bottom writhed a small sand rattlesnake.

Suddenly Tignal Jones looked up and saw Carmody. There was a play, then, which only Carmody and Jones and Bannerman were aware of.

Jones grinned and wiped his thumb down the side of his nose. A man of seventy, he wore a dirty imperial and a mustache the color of an old rug. His shirt was a faded blue army blouse with a sergeant's chevrons. He had leased his ranch for twelve years to Bannerman, which enabled him to live in town, drink all he liked, gamble, and brag of women he had known.

There was his grin, and Tom's wink; and at once a hard bolt of suspicion ran through Bannerman's face. That was all.

Tig prodded Bannerman's shoulder, across the table. "Whack up!" he said.

"Double or nothing," insisted Bannerman, thumping the table.

Creed transferred his hand to Carmody's shoulder for support. He had apparently spent a good part of his advance wages in the saloon. "The old ripstover's taken him five times running! He come in a bit ago with that contraption and bet Bannerman he couldn't hold his hand against the glass when the snake struck."

Tig Jones fingered his imperial, squinting over the proposition of doubling his winnings or losing them. Someone said, "Take 'er, Tig!" Carmody saw Bannerman glance up at Wiley. The ramrod grubbed in his pocket and handed him a sack of makings. Bannerman began to roll a cigarette.

"Double or nothing, Tig!" he insisted again. "Come on . . ."

The old man looked up at Carmody and his eye closed in a slow wink. He said, "I'll go it."

Morgan Wiley uttered a disgusted sound. He turned and shoved through the crowd to the bar.

Suddenly it was quiet. A man behind Carmody thrust against him to get a better view. Bannerman lighted the cigarette and let it hang in his lips. His face was corrugated with deep lines. His eyes were intent. He gripped the neck of the jug with one hand and watched the sand-rattler weave slowly back and forth with glints of a red threadlike tongue. There was the faintest hiss of rattles through the rawhide. Slowly Bannerman put his palm against the glass. His mouth firmed.

The snake struck, making a soft sound against the glass. Bannerman's hand was a foot away. The men shouted.

Holt Bannerman swore softly and looked at his hand. He took the cigarette from his lips. "Tig," he said, "they ought to have you in a bottle, too. You're a menace to God-fearing people." Shaking his head, he counted out five double-eagles.

The old man jingled them. "I'll stand drinks at the bar," he said to the grinning punchers around the table. "Tom, you set with me."

As the crowd thinned, Tom introduced Creed. "Creed's going to help out on my place for a spell," he told Jones.

"Don't know what you aim to do with an extra hand on a spread the size of yours," Tig declared.

Bannerman was losing his good humor. The long vertical creases of his face deepened. "Tig, I'd like to see you outside for a minute," he said.

"What's the matter with right here?"

"I said outside."

"I say go to hell," Tig snapped.

Carmody smiled and watched Bannerman, but the rancher regarded Tig almost without emotion, measuring him through a long instant. Jones presently turned his attention to Carmody.

"Tom, I hear you've got a power of Shorthorn cattle down at the station."

"Two hundred and fifty head."

"Know they'll winter-kill, don't you?"

"They're long-two's from a cold country. I figure they'll tough it out."

Jones shrugged. "Just one thing I don't figger," he said. "What are you going to feed 'em on?"

"Grass."

"What grass?" Tig grinned maliciously.

Carmody looked closely at him. He had a sharp and sudden recollection of Laura's warning, but he kept his voice dry, saying, "Any I can rustle," and looked for a barman.

With an impatient gesture, Bannerman moved his chair and rose. "Tig, I haven't got time to fool away here. I want to fix up our lease. It was up for renewal ten days ago. I've been trying to catch you."

"What lease?" Jones slyly winked at Tom, and relief poured down through Carmody like cold water.

"A joke is a joke," Bannerman snapped. "Come outside."

Tig Jones had a drink in his hand. With no warning at all, he threw it in Bannerman's face.

It caught Bannerman with his arm half-raised.

The whiskey struck his forehead and ran down over his face. He stood there, stunned. It was silent around the table until Bannerman swore. Throwing his chair aside, he lunged after the old man.

Suddenly he stopped. Jones had drawn a long-barreled Navy pistol. He was on his feet, prodding it into Bannerman's belly, his face purplish. He looked crazy at that instant, thought Tom—as crazy as they said he was.

—4—

WITH THE BARREL of the gun, Tig Jones kept prodding
Bannerman back. His face had a greasy shine in the glow
of the coal-oil lamps. His eyes glistened, and Tom thought
that if there was a pattern for madness, it was an old man
in a ruined army uniform with a Colt in his hand.

"They'd thank me from one end of Union County to the
other," said Tig, "if this thing was to go off. I'll bet they
couldn't even pick a jury to convict me!" He kept walking
forward, pushing Bannerman back.

At a pool table where the voices had not reached,
someone broke the balls with a crack. Carmody watched
Bannerman's face. It was hard and set, yet without fear.
Bannerman knew he was standing face to face with death,
but he was too proud, too arrogant, to show it.

Jones was talking viciously through set teeth. "You've
kept me from a right price for twelve years by daring
anybody to take Snaketrack away from you. You knew I
was too old and liquor-logged to ranch it myself. But I've
got a new customer. I'm through punying around with
you. You can hold them summer herds right where they
are. They ain't going back on Snaketrack!"

Bannerman looked at the gun, at the flaccid, unhealthy
features of the rancher. "Aren't they?" he snapped. "When
a man's leased a piece of land for twelve years, he's
earned the right to a warning before he's put off it."

"All right," said Tig. "Call this a warning. Stay off
Snaketrack."

Bannerman's jaws ridged with muscle. "I've got two

26

herds coming off summer pasture next week. Fifteen hundred cows. I've rested that land for them all summer. They're going back, Tig.''

Jones slowly shook his head, still grinning, savoring the moment. With careless movement he put the gun away. "It don't matter to me whether you ate the grass yourself or saved it for Tom Carmody's cattle. You and me are through.'' Then he looked at Carmody, saying, "This is your answer, Tom, in case you were wonderin'. I reckoned it wouldn't hurt you to go back and forth over it a spell. You'll enjoy the land that much more.''

Tom smiled, but his attention was still on Bannerman. The rancher was staring at Jones, his face taut, his mouth sealed. Tig turned the bottle with both hands but yanked one hand away as the snake struck.

"Bucktooth,'' he chuckled. "I'm going to be more careful about the friends I make, next time! The ones with pizen in 'em, I'm going to keep them in a jug, like you. . . . Well, let's you and I go along to Brophy's place and win us a couple more drinks.''

Then, for a moment, he turned back to Carmody. "There she is, Tom. Meet me at my shack in the morning. Once I get the money, she's yours.''

With the bottle under his arm, he paced along the bar, a lean, untidy old man whose face cherished the knowledge that he had just put a barrel of gunpowder under Union County.

Carmody watched Bannerman stare at the doors after Tig had departed. After a moment the rancher took a cigar from his pocket and bit the end off it. He spat out the nubbin of tobacco and turned toward Carmody. He looked at him as though preparing to say something, but presently walked to the bar. Several of his men stood there. They seemed embarrassed, for there was nothing to say. If anyone should speak, it was Bannerman, but his thinking ran too deep for speech. He was caught with over a thousand cattle, and winter was being made tonight. . . .

Creed was watching Bannerman with a grin. "He ain't so tough!'' he said.

Carmody shook his head. "If you weren't drunk, you'd

be thinking clearer than that. Save enough out of that money for smoking tobacco. We'll leave out tomorrow afternoon for Snaketrack. Try to be sober.''

Resting his cheek against his hand, Creed smiled fuzzily. "I ain't drunk, Tom, just tired. I been setting up with a sick cow for three days.''

"And somebody's going to be setting up with a sick cowboy tomorrow," Tom said. "I'm going to see to the cattle, now. I won't need you.''

The street was full of the hiss of water and the gurgle of downspouts. Through slanting lines of rain, he walked to the station. Standing among sodden trees, he could see a lantern moving in quick arcs between the loading pens and the cattle cars. The lantern halted. There was a thudding of hoofs as it was hung against a car. Then metal clinked under a hammer.

Carmody strode past the station. It was dark. The agent had gone home. Tom's palm pressed his thigh; he thought of the Colt lying in the bottom of his grip. Down the line of reeking cattle cars a man was working with a lock. Tom was on the point of leaving the loading platform when someone rose from behind a red fire-barrel.

He saw at once that it was Chunk McAllister. Chunk's fists were bunched. He said, "Don't go down there, Tom.''

Anger bolted savagely through Tom. "You drink too many men's liquor, Chunk. You don't know where your loyalty belongs any more. You've drunk mine tonight and now you're on Bannerman's. Get out of my way.''

The bounty hunter hunched his sprawling shoulders. "I'm working for Bannerman, Tom, not you.''

Carmody snapped his knee up in a feint at Chunk's crotch, and as the man twisted away he slammed his fist full into his face. Chunk went to his knees and fell face down. Carmody jumped across him and ran forward. He slithered in the mud, caught himself and went on. As he passed the second car, a man jumped from the coupling to land before him. An arm came down in a hand-axing arc. A brakeman's bar glistened, and Carmody swerved away and smashed the edge of his fist into Jim Shaniko's face.

The moment was brief and savage.

Tom felt a dull explosion of pain in his right shoulder as the bar landed. He tried to raise his fist, but his arm was dead. He saw the club rise again and got his shoulder into the wet, bleeding face and crowded the Cross Anchor range boss back against the car. The club struck above his kidneys. He cried out, and the gaunt, rocky face close to his grimaced. The deep-socketed eyes, dull as stone, watched him slip down.

Someone else was running up the line. Carmody struggled up, gasping.

There was an instant of full comprehension. He saw the empty car at the end of the string, and from somewhere he heard the deep bawling of an injured cow. It was suddenly intolerable to him that these cattle of his should be dumped from the cars and turned into the freezing rain.

As Wiley came on, Carmody clawed his right hand into Shaniko's face. Cursing, Shaniko stumbled aside, clinging to Tom's arm. Morg Wiley came up then, swerving in to slug Tom in the face. Tom floundered back into the bars of the pen.

Blood was pouring from a cut above his eye. With his sleeve he wiped it away. He was seized with a violent impulse to smash Wiley to his knees. He lurched away from the barrier, his fist cocked; but at that moment he saw Wiley's hand come from under his coat. Carmody halted, seeing the dark gleam of a revolver, and in Wiley's face a headlong anger. He had the thought: *This isn't over cattle or Snaketrack—it's over Ruth!* And for the first time, he knew how bitterly Wiley hated him for having taken Ruth from him.

They stood there, and no one moved and no one spoke. Big Jim Shaniko waited with the brakeman's bar resting on his shoulder. Tom heard frightened cattle thrusting against the sides of the cattle-cars, the sizzling of raindrops against the hot peak of the lantern. He knew what was going on in the ramrod's mind. He was trying to push himself into firing the gun.

Wiley spoke, suddenly. "Get a rope, Jim. *Andale!*"

Shaniko turned and strode up the grade toward the

station. When Wiley stirred, the dark wedge of his shoulders tilting forward, a stream of rainwater ran from his troughed hatbrim. The gun's steady eye did not waver.

"Maybe I can get some answers now, Tom," he said. "How about it—did you marry Ruth in El Paso?"

"This is a hell of a time to talk about women," Tom grunted. His jaws worked. "Wiley, if you unload those cattle, I'll—"

Anger came up in his throat like bile, choking him, because he knew Wiley was going ahead and nothing but a gun would stop him.

Wiley's brows arched, then drew down in a savage frown. "We're not talking about cattle now. And we're talking about one woman. Are you married to Ruth? Damn you if you lie to me."

"To hell with you, Wiley," Tom said wearily. "But I'm not married to anybody."

Wiley studied him a long time, his small, irate eyes squinting. "If she comes back, you'd better not act like you were aiming to marry her, either. You got me, Tom?"

"What makes you think she'll come back?"

Something relieved, something sly, came into Wiley's face. It had not been there a moment earlier. "If she ain't married to you," he said, "she'll be back. Sooner or later. Because Ruth ain't going to walk out for good on anything like Cross Anchor."

Tom smiled, seeing the shabby line of the ramrod's thinking. "And you'll be the fair-haired boy when she comes home, eh? The bull of the woods. Bannerman's pick for a son-in-law—because you stuck by him when I ran out. Morg," he said, amused but earnest, "you couldn't make a bigger mistake than make a play for Ruth. Bannerman would can you quick as he did me. Because nobody will ever be good enough for Ruth Bannerman; not in the old man's eyes. The man she marries will own Cross Anchor one day. And believe me, it won't be a sixty-a-month ramrod who tips his hat too much."

"Shut up, Tom," Wiley said softly. "Don't open your mouth again. Or you'll get the butt of this gun in your teeth."

Shaniko came trotting back with a coil of rope, his boots chopping wetly in the soaked gravel. When Wiley said, "Turn around and stand against the pen," Carmody did so. He stood there while Wiley vaulted the bars. "Put your arms through the slats," Wiley said. Tom hesitated, but Wiley pressed the gun against his spine and he did as he had been ordered.

Shaniko kinked his arms up and lashed his wrists to the two-by-twelve. He tied his ankles to a lower bar and stood back. Tom could see the wide grin on the range boss's face. He was swinging the free end of the excess rope.

"How do you like gringo poker, General?" he asked. "With a couple of gringos stacking the deck?"

Blood was coagulating in Tom's eye; blood was salty in his mouth. His mouth pursed and he spat at him. Shaniko swung the rope and cut angrily at his face. Closing his eyes, Tom turned his head and felt the manila against his ear.

Wiley moved his sloping shoulders. "It ain't that we're in any hurry to see you starve out, Tom, but we wanted to be sure you didn't think we were afraid of you. This is just in case you had any such notion. . . ."

Suddenly Tom asked, "Is this on your own, or did Bannerman send you?"

"This is for the old man," Wiley said. Then he glanced at Shaniko. "Jim, go get a few boys. We'd best be at this." After Shaniko left, Wiley walked on down the line and began rigging the loading chute into place before the first car.

After about fifteen minutes Shaniko was back with a half-dozen cowboys in jackets and slickers. There was still a small head of steam in the freight engine which had brought the cars up. Carmody was aware of a shovel grating in coal, and after a while the train made a couple of crashing retreats down the tracks until the door of a car was lined up with the loading chute.

The work went rapidly. The Shorthorns were prodded down the chute and run toward the river. After a car was emptied, another gate was opened in the maze of the pens and cattle were run up the chute. When the door banged shut, a cowboy in the engine backed the string until the next car was presented.

Carmody's hands and legs were icy, the circulation choked by the ropes. He rested his forehead against a plank and tried to think, and then tried not to. He had ten thousand dollars in these cattle. They were short-legged animals and not made for rocky country. No cow was made for running across a river mined with rocks, and Carmody could hear cattle bawling on the far side of the stream.

Then, after a long while, it was finished, and he watched the train back off into the darkness, moving toward the main line five miles out on the prairie. The voices of punchers faintly drifted back from the river, where the cattle were being driven across.

Tom was alone. He began shouting, but his voice was drowned in hissing rain. In sudden fury, he lunged back, yanking savagely at the ropes. He strained until his face corded, but then he knew it was useless, and he groaned and slumped against the barrier.

Much later, he was aware of a man walking in the gravel. Stiff with cold, he roused to stare up the tracks toward the station. A man was shambling along in a slicker. Looking closely, Carmody called abruptly:

"Creed!"

Creed Davis stopped. He peered ahead. Then he came on at a loose hurried walk. He stopped behind him and said, "Tom, what the hell you doin'? Where's a' cattle?"

There was rage and craziness in Tom. He closed his eyes and made himself stand without moving. "I'm tied," he said. "The cattle are gone. Get out a knife and cut these ropes."

Creed said, slowly, "My God, Tom. You mean—"

"Cut the ropes!" Tom shouted suddenly.

Davis fumbled a pocket knife out of his pocket and cut the wet manila. When Tom stepped back, his legs caved under him and he went onto his hands and knees. Creed began drunkenly trying to help him, but Tom swore and got to his feet. He held to the bar of the pen as he walked toward the station, feeling the circulation move hotly through

32

his limbs. He stopped under the wide overhang of the station building. He was soaked to the skin, his face stiff with cold. In the faint glow of a night light inside the station, Creed squinted at him.

"My God, Tom! You—your eye . . ."

Tom doggedly shook his head. He started up the path to the street. "Did Wiley come back to the saloon before you left?"

"I ain't seen him. I was there till about three."

Tom walked fast, fists swinging. Creed unsteadily tried to keep up. "What happened, Tom? Where's all the cattle?"

"I caught Wiley beginning to unload them. Wiley held a gun on me while Shaniko tied me up. Then they went ahead."

Creed's voice broke. "And I was drinking whiskey on your money while they done it! So help me, Tom!"

"So help Wiley," Tom said savagely. "So help him God when I catch up with him!"

They reached the dark livery stable. Tom halted, wondering if Bailey, the liveryman, or a hostler would be around. He decided to get into dry clothing and secure a gun before rousing the stable, and he went on down the glistening boardwalk. The small hotel-lobby was dimly-lit, a clock ticking loudly behind the counter. The clerk was asleep with his head on a newspaper. They went down the hall to Tom's room, entered and lighted a lamp.

Tom stripped off his clothes and peeled his underwear to the waist, standing before the mirror to look at himself. He looked lean as rawhide, but with a springiness to his arms and shoulders. His face was smeared with blood, and for an instant, less because of the blood than for the crazy fury in it, he did not recognize himself. He swore softly. Creed watched him with melancholy self-accusation. Looking at himself, a little pulse of common-sense started to throb in Carmody, and the stiffness went out of him and fatigue flowed through him, as enervating as a warm bath. He knew then that he was in no shape to go man-hunting. He was exhausted. He was drunk on an anger that could only lead him into tragic blunders.

33

Creed said, "What are you going to do about Wiley, Tom?"

Tom turned wearily and poured water into the flowered china basin. "I don't know," he said, honestly. "But when I get through with him, he'll know I've done something."

—5—

HE DID NOT awaken until nine.

When he looked out the window, he saw a clear, cold daylight. A horse grazed in the vacant lot next to the hotel. A freezing wind had risen; he heard it secretly trying the casement of the window.

He woke Creed, who set his teeth against the misery of his hangover, and dressed. From his suitcase, Tom extracted his Colt and belted it on. His rage had settled out bright and thin and sharp. He thought of the cattle with broken legs lying in the stream. Of the days of brush-popping before the last of the unhurt cows would be rounded up. And more than formally sealing the Snaketrack lease, even, he wanted to square things with Wiley.

They went out, the two of them, and ate at a lunch counter next to Hurley's Gun-Shop. With the food and coffee warm in him, Tom's anticipation rose, sleek and strong. He grinned at Creed. "Go down to Bailey's," he told the puncher, "and rent us a couple of good rock-horses. I'll stop by a couple of places and meet you there. Then we'll go cow-hunting."

Creed scowled. "Wait a minute, Tom—"

Tom settled his Stetson and walked into the street.

Soledad was wide awake, the last store open, the green blinds rolled up even in the bank's front windows. Horses and buggies roiled the muddy street. A gang of cowboys whooped in from a side street with a small and skinny herd from the upper Cimarron, and he watched them pass. Other men rode out, back to the hard work of preparing for winter, of cutting stove wood for line shacks, repairing drift fence moving trusses of hay to the spots where blizzard-pushed cattle drifted.

But he did not see Wiley's nor Shaniko's ponies on the street. He glanced along each hitchrack. He was convinced they would still be in town, with Bannerman's big beef-herd shipped and a lag of a day or two before the next bunch of steers was brought in.

He crossed the street and approached the Great Western Barn. A man standing by the broken adobe corner of the saloon struck a match for his pipe; it seemed almost like a signal. Tom inspected him closely as he walked, and suddenly recognized him. It was Marshal Mike Ridge.

Ridge smiled and said in feigned surprise, "Why, howdy, Tom! You been boycotting me?"

"You were next on my list of calls," Tom said.

"It's fine you're back," said Ridge, giving his large hard-palmed hand. He was a gaunt, tough-eyed man of about forty.

"Keeping you busy?" asked Tom.

"Not too busy, up to now. How is it with you?"

"I'll be pushed to beat snow," Tom told him. ". . . You knew I'm ranching again?"

"I'd heard." Ridge brushed his mustache with the cuff of his mackinaw—Tom had forgotten the gesture. The mustache had always seemed essential to the part he played—the strong, fearless Buffalo Bill sort of lawman. He wore yellow cowhide boots, his black pants tucked into them, a belted gray mackinaw, and pinned his marshal's shield to his round-crowned Stetson. Tom put his hand out again and said, "Well, I'll probably see you around."

"What's your hurry? Let's have a drink."

"Another time, Mike. I'm looking for somebody."

Ridge's eyes were steady and wise, and he smiled. "I know who you're looking for. But he ain't there. Why don't you get the warpaint off your face and simmer down? It's the same old town—Bannerman's town, in lots of things. No use trying to change that all at once."

"I already have," Tom told him. "Tig Jones has leased Snaketrack to me."

Ridge did not seem surprised nor impressed. "I heard about it," he said. "Of course, he's been liquor-logged so long you never know whether he'll go prove up on anything he says or not."

"He'll prove up on this," Tom declared. Yet he searched the marshal's face quickly to see whether anything lay behind the remark.

"Well, I hope so. The town needs a change. But don't count too much on Tig—or on Bannerman setting up and begging, either."

"Bannerman," Tom told him flatly, "is just another cowman, and nobody will ever tell me any different."

Again the marshal made the mustache-stroking gesture. "It looks," he said, glancing at the cut over Tom's eye, "as though somebody already had. You didn't have to have that scrap. You could have let Bannerman load his cattle. Why didn't you?"

"Because it was raining and I didn't want to chance broken legs."

The marshal smiled. "And maybe because Bannerman told you you had to unload, eh?"

Tom shrugged. "Maybe."

He said that and started toward the door of the saloon, but the marshal said, "They ain't in there, Tom. None of 'em."

"I'll look for myself."

Ridge came after him, half-angrily. "Do you have to make things tough all around? Swear out a complaint against Wiley, if you think you've been wronged. Assault and battery—I don't know what else you could claim."

"I claim," Tom said, "that I can handle it myself."

Ridge's eyes thinned. "Billy the Kid was only twenty when he killed his last man," he said. "You're too old to set a record even if you started today. I've always thought you were a smart lad. Let me keep on thinking so, and not have to go after you with a posse."

"Like you did Pete Trinidad?" Tom asked wickedly.

Ridge lifted his shoulders. "Every man makes a mistake. Trinidad was mine."

". . . And Jim Shaniko's. Shaniko claimed he caught

37

him with a running iron in his boot. You backed him up in court. You were a hell of a time admitting the running iron might have been intended to repair a wagon, instead of brand a cow, as Pete claimed. You were a little slow remembering about Pete and Jim being in love with the same girl, too.''

And for some reason he thought of Laura. He thought, *If I were in love with Laura, and Ridge knew it, he'd make me as much trouble as Shaniko made Trinidad.*

"Shaniko was doing his job," Ridge insisted. "He thought Trinidad was the cow-thief I was looking for, and he had a deputy's badge to bring him in. Blame me for the rest."

"I do," Tom assured him. "I'm going into the Great Western now. There isn't any ordinance against a man having a drink, is there?"

Ridge's face was mean when he had been pushed; it was hard with dislike now. "There ain't an ordinance against it so long as you don't have to shoot anybody doing it," he stated. "If I were you, I'd keep away from Wiley for a while."

Tom knew he had the marshal off-balance, and he had a desire to nettle him further. "Maybe I ought to keep away from Laura Cincinnatus too, eh?" he grinned.

Ridge gave Tom a look which made him sorry he had made the remark. His eyes were grave, and his manner had become very quiet; a man would need to be blind not to perceive that the marshal was in love with Laura.

"I thought maybe I could help you, Tom," Ridge said. "You're into something pretty serious, whether you know it or not. If you start bringing Laura into it, you can be damned sure you won't find me breaking my neck to help you."

It was in Tom's mind to apologize, but at once the marshal ducked his head in a curt nod and turned up the walk. Tom watched him walk away, thinking, *Why did I say that?* There was a logical answer to it. That he was jealous of Laura's interest in Ridge. *Jealous of a girl I've known half my life,* he thought. But that only half-refuted the testimony, and he was frowning when he turned back to the frosted glass doors of the saloon.

He hesitated a moment, and then parted the doors and walked inside. The room was thinly populated with men stealing an early drink before hurrying on to work. Tom stood under the inspection of them, a hard and limber-looking man with a dark bruised face. Then he went forward to stand at the short elbow of the bar, looking down its polished length. Murphy, the proprietor, came forward, wiping a beer glass.

"Seen Morg Wiley?" Tom asked.

Murphy breathed against the side of the stein and polished it vigorously. "Ain't seen any Cross Anchor boys, Tom."

"Where would they be?"

"You have to ask Bannerman."

"Where's he?"

"Don't know, Tom," Red Murphy smiled.

Suddenly the tension left Tom, and he gave Murphy a grin. "Saloon man's ethics, eh? Give me a pint, Red. I've got a boy that needs a hair or two of the dog that bit him."

Before Bailey's Livery, Creed Davis waited with two horses saddled with deep mountain rigs. After setting his stirrups, Tom mounted and they rode north from town. There was a skim of ice on the puddles in the open land beyond the gaunt family-orchards. An old Mexican, driving a small band of milk goats, called a greeting to them.

They found where the Shorthorns had been driven across the river, and a short distance downstream a cow lay in the stiff, rimed weeds at the edge of the stream. A muscle bunched in Tom's jaw. "One . . ." he said.

They crossed through rocky shallows and lunged up the raw new bank created by last night's storm. Nearby they discovered two more cows, both living, both with broken fore-legs. Tom looked down at them, drew his Colt and pulled the hammer back. The shot exploded in the cold air; the smoke whipped away like a gray rag. "Two," he said, and he quieted the pony and moved up to the next cow. He shot it through the eye. "Three. A hundred and twenty dollars. Out of Morg Wiley's—'' He set his jaws and spurred on into the dwarf junipers and piñon.

For an hour, working up the long toe of the mesa, they saw no more cattle. Topping out on the vast table sweeping back to the mountains, they saw two herds coming out of the foothills, one of them being driven south, the other north, toward lower winter pastures. Tom began picking out other flashes of horns in the tough half-sized forest. The Shorthorns had been driven deeply toward the hills and scattered. Creed sighed.

"I ain't complaining, Tom, but this is going to take a week, workin' alone."

"I know. I'll rustle a couple of boys that know these hills. Any you find while I'm gone, push them south. The boys will bring blankets and chuck, so stay with it."

"When are you coming back?" Creed asked.

"Later. I've got to get Tig Jones sober enough to sign a paper, and that may take all day."

—— **6** ——

IN HIS MIND, now he traced in black strokes, like the marks a roundup foreman made on a tally board, the things that were ahead, the moves that could not wait.

Snaketrack.

There was nothing more important than getting an old man's flimsy signature on a piece of paper. *"I, Tignal Jones, for ten dollars and certain other considerations . . ."* For these considerations he would open the door to the gold-and-lavender basin called Snaketrack—a country foreign to the cold, reluctant highlands, an all-year range a thousand feet below the high plateaus. Even Bannerman owned no land like this. The best cows he sold each year were the ones he had primed on his Snaketrack lease.

But winter was as close as the next storm—it might be in that high haze moving up behind the Sangre de Cristos now—and Tom had four times the cattle his own up-and-down ranch could support for three months. Over them hung the menace of unfinished business.

He had a draft for eighteen thousand dollars in his valise at the hotel. He remembered the time Banker Phil Cornelius would not lend him seventy-five dollars, that first winter. "Tom, this country is full of good cowboys bent on going broke as bad ranchers." . . . He wondered how Cornelius would look when he read the check. And he found he did not care.

It was there—the foundation under him he had always dreamed of. It was there, and now it was a go-to-hell strength in him. He did not care what Cornelius thought,

41

whether he thought he had stolen the money or won it in a poker game. The money was there, and the banker would read his name on a check and perhaps set his teeth as he paid off on it—but he would pay.

Entering Soledad in the early afternoon, he saw a girl hurrying across the street with pertly-swinging skirts, a red shawl over her head. It was Laura. He compared her with the girl who had almost been his wife. There was about the difference that there was between a runaway team and a lifey team in hand. Ruth Bannerman would always get what she wanted when she wanted it. Laura would get what she wanted, too—but not until she made her man want her to have it.

Tom rode to the bank. Phil Cornelius had not come back from lunch, but he opened an account with a check on his bank in El Paso. He went out again into the freezing wind. The rent pony stood with its back humped in the cold. Tom gazed down the street, filling himself with the look of the town, thinking, *When I come from the judge's, this will be a different town.* It would be different because he would view it with new perspective. Out of the signing of a piece of paper would emerge something steady and sure—something to replace the hot excitement of the mood in which he had come back to Soledad.

Laura let him into the bright little parlor with its Indian rugs and tawny plastered walls. The first thing he thought, absorbing the order and cheerfulness, was, *A man needs something like this!* He had spent his adult life in line-shacks and bunkhouses, homes with the cold comforts of a cave. But entering this parlor was like going into a woman's arms.

Laura was exceptionally neat and pretty in a green gown with small white flowers, a gown with no flourishes but some strategic tucks. It flattered her bosom, hugged her waist, and gained fullness as it swept to the floor. Her black hair, which had been in pigtails when he left, was up in a chignon now, and she wore small turquoise earrings and a chatelaine watch. She had the look of a woman who knew she looked well—composed and a trifle aloof.

Tom regarded her with the smiling speculation a man

has for a woman flimsily barricaded in her feminity. *I wonder what she'd do if I picked her up and kissed her?* he thought. Then he realized she must have seen something of this in his face, for she glanced quickly away.

"I'm sorry about your cattle, Tom," she said. "We heard what happened last night."

Tom sailed his hat onto an antelope prong. "It could have been worse. I only lost three cows. And a week's work rounding them up, before I'm through."

"Couldn't it have been better, though?" Laura asked. "Why didn't you let Bannerman load his cattle?"

"You're beginning to sound like Ridge," Tom remarked. "Papoose, one way to make sure a man doesn't do what you want is to tell him he's got to. That's what Bannerman told me. So I wouldn't unload them."

He was half-joking, but she looked stiff and unhappy. Turning to the window, she looked down on the rusty tin roof of the feed store. For some reason he thought of Mike Ridge—smoothing his yellow mustache in this parlor after kissing her. He wondered if it had progressed that far, and he frowned and picked up a small Indian grinding-bowl and put it down.

"Have you seen Tig this morning?" Laura asked.

Something in her tone chilled him. He glanced quickly at her. "Not yet," he said. "I've been out cow-hunting all morning. Why?"

"He was here about an hour ago, but he got thirsty waiting for you, and left. He won't be hard to find. I—I hope you'll tie it up with him quickly."

Still Tom watched her, as she turned. "That's what I'm here for. . . . Is the judge busy?"

"He's with Clance Harper, right now. Do you remember Clance?"

Tom remembered him at once—a middle-aged cowboy who had been on Bannerman's ranch as long as he could remember—a man who ran more to tallow than to youth.

"Sure I remember him," he told her. "Is he still on Cross Anchor?"

Speculation was coming into Laura's eyes, and now she smiled curiously and said, "No—he was fired just after

43

you left. He's been trying to raise hay ever since. But I think he's lost out there, too. Tom," she said, "do you want to do something for me?"

Tom smiled, trying to read her. "I might," he said.

"Hire Clance as a puncher," she said eagerly. "Oh, I know he's not young, and he's a little heavy, but—"

"But you want me to hire him anyway," Tom chuckled; and then he said, "So I'll hire him."

He had from Laura a look of beaming approval, and he took her chin in his thumb and forefinger and said, "Some day, Laura, your kids will knock themselves out shoveling snow off the walk for a look like that. What's this between you and Clance?"

"It's just that I feel sorry for him—being out of work, and all."

There were footfalls inside the office and the porcelain knob turned, the door opening slightly. A man said gruffly, "Well, Judge, I'll think about it. Thank you, Judge . . ."

A stout, middle-aged man in denim trousers and a red plaid shirt came from the office. Seeing Laura, he took off his hat again. He was too heavy for a cow-puncher, a heavy-limbed, powerful man with thick gray hair and a florid face.

"Remember Tom Carmody?" Laura said quickly to him. "He was another Cross Anchor man who had the good sense to quit."

Harper grinned. "It don't always take good sense, Laura. It just takes forty pounds too much weight; and then you might let a couple of day-herds blow up on roundup, and it's all fixed, you ain't working for Cross Anchor any more."

Laura said proudly, "I wish you could see the timothy and broom Clance raised this summer!"

Carmody asked him where he was ranching, and Harper said, "You remember the old Ryan place? It was Bannerman's homestead, you know. He got his start there, but I got my finish. When he canned me he said I could buy this piece of land from him for a couple of dollars down and the rest out of crops."

He hesitated, and Tom saw him remembering the days

and weeks of stump-grubbing, of clearing brush by hand, of leveling and plowing.

"But when I got the hay off," Harper said, "he decided he didn't need it. It'd been an early winter. And there was a lot of swamp hay in it, so it's not worth shipping. He filed foreclosure papers last week."

"Sold the hay yet?" Tom asked quickly.

Harper looked at Laura, then back at Tom, his face clouding oddly. "Tom, would you a'bought it?"

"I'll pay cash right now. Maybe you can fool Bannerman yet!"

"Well, that's fine," Clance Harper said bitterly. "That's just fine. Only I just burnt it all," he said, and he walked past them to the door and tore it open to go out onto the landing.

Laura cried, "Clance, you wait!" and hurried after him.

Someone was in the office doorway, then, a stout, old man in a brown, velvet-collared box coat. Broad-shouldered and gray, Judge Myron Cincinnatus always made Tom think of an old badger. He smiled wryly and said, "That's what folks have been trying to tell you, Tom. Bannerman can give a fox cards and spades and come off with his brush. Come on in."

—7—

WITH AN EXTENSION lamp shining above him, abetting the dull afternoon light, the office acquired character. Things did not lend the judge character, Tom reflected; he bestowed it on them. He was grubbing in his desk for something, a revolving bookcase at his elbow, a clock ticking loudly in the abdomen of a bronze Venus atop the desk. The room seemed mellow, cured in the smoke of a thousand cigars, and over everything, like a fine dust, there had settled a luster of patience and long-thinking. It was on the rows of cowhide law books, on the letter-press and the safe, something so personal that it seemed to Tom they would have to be buried with him.

Cincinnatus found what he wanted, a box filled with fragments of cigars, clipped off when he was interrupted in a smoke. He lighted one and sighed.

"Tom, you're the first right thing about this week. It was time you came back where you belonged. Going to stay a while?"

"I figure to," Tom said. Looking around the dusky room, he felt a sense of rightness—as though he belonged here, where so often he had absorbed advice from the judge. And yet he wondered whether he was the same man he had been when he went away—the kind of man who could take advice which started with a quotation from the Bible, percolated down through Blackstone, and came out as a single word of patience.

The judge smiled at him through lavender cigar smoke. "So you're going to whip Bannerman like a youngster,"

46

he said. "And so was Clance. Well, he's fooled a lot of them."

Touched with annoyance, Tom said, "I'm not dealing with Bannerman. I'm dealing with Tig Jones—a drunk and a fool, maybe, but isn't his signature as good as the next man's?"

"Every bit. After you get it."

"All right," Tom said shortly. "Then that's what I'm here to get."

Nodding, Cincinnatus tilted back and let the stout spring of the chair support him. "I talked to Tig this morning. He's still willing. In fact, he's anxious to close it up today, take his money and go to San Francisco to see that new grandson of his. And when Tig gets an idea, it's next door to being done."

"You didn't get his signature?"

"How could I, until I got your money?" Cincinnatus pulled a paper from his desk. "Here's how the lease reads. At seven cents an acre, you owe Tig five thousand, two hundred fifty dollars annual rent. The lease is for five years, the first year in advance. Effort to be made to keep out rattleweed, varmints, and so forth. All right?"

"All right," Tom smiled. He had a feeling of calmness, and a strange desire—that he might have been able to tell that other Tom Carmody that it was going to come out all right. It might have made his last year less grim, less productive of the hard-jawed cocksureness that bothered Laura. But today those things were Tom Carmody.

Cincinnatus took off his steel spectacles and massaged his eyes. "Let's see the color of your money."

"It's downstairs. I'll give you a check as soon as you give me a pen."

Cincinnatus lowered his hand. "Did you open that account with a cashier's check?"

"No. It was a personal check on my bank in El Paso." He inspected the lawyer with sudden sharpness, a quick worry. "What's the matter with that?"

Cincinnatus replaced the spectacles, but for a moment he did not reply. . . . "Tom, Cornelius won't pay on that check till the money comes up from El Paso. And of course, as Tig Jones' trustee, I can't let you have the land until my client gets the money."

A strong pulse broke loose in Tom. "Cut it out, Judge! Cornelius can wire for an okay on the money."

"But he doesn't have to pay until the money gets here! You see, there's the matter of offending his biggest stockholder, and I don't need to tell you who that is."

For the moment, Tom's shock had no voice. He thought of Tig, capricious and reliable as a drunken Apache. He thought of Bannerman, going to work on the news that Tom was stalled.

Taking a key from the desk, Cincinnatus inserted it in the abdomen of the bronze Venus and began to wind the clock.

"In fact, Tom, you might say you've been a little hasty. I wish you'd taken me into your confidence about this sooner. I'm anxious to settle with Tig while he's in the mood, because—well, you know how Tig is. But any way you look at it, right now you're just another rancher with too many cattle and no place to put them. And that's how it's got to be until I see the money here on my desk."

From the window, Tom gazed down on the bleak main street. Leaves whirled along to a rendezvous in a ditch. The manes and tails of horses streamed in the wind, and in everything he saw there was coldness and melancholy. In the silence, Judge Cincinnatus' pen scratched.

"Tom," he said, "don't take this personally, will you? If I approved the lease without the cash, Bannerman's lawyer could have me disbarred. I would think a little caution might have been what would have helped most."

Tom plucked a racked arrow from the wall. "I've been cautious all my life. The most it ever got me was fifty a month as Bannerman's range boss. After I got impatient, I began to make money. Look at the Indian who used this arrow—he knew when to squat on his heels, and when to saddle and ride."

"That particular arrow belonged to an Injun who was more of a man to saddle and ride than to squat on his heels. We hung him at Fort Union last winter."

48

The door opened. Laura stood there, her smile quickly giving way to anxiety. "What is it, Tom?"

Her father sighed, "I've had to put Tom off for a while, Laura. It seems his money is in El Paso."

Laura regarded him silently. "But will Tig wait?" She said that and then turned to Tom. "Oh, Tom, I wish—I wish you'd written Dad what you were going to do! All you really seem to know is that you're going to humiliate Bannerman the way he humiliated you! And you overlook everything else."

"That's a good enough ambition, isn't it?" Tom said.

"Revenge isn't ambition," the judge said sharply. "It's gunpowder. You blow things up with gunpowder. You build things with ambition. . . . What about this money, when it gets here?" he demanded. "Where'd you get it?"

Tom looked at him, then at Laura, then out the window. "Mexico."

"Gambling?" Cincinnatus asked.

"No, I—" He frowned at Laura, and shrugged. "I suppose she might as well know. She'll make our lives miserable until she does. I made some of it as a cattle-buyer for Lopez-Montezuma's rebel army. They gave Diaz a run for a while. I'd take off with a bag of money and bring back a herd of gringo beef. Last June I left with thirty thousand dollars. I was in El Paso when the rebels were cornered near Chihuahua City. I put the money in the bank and went down to see what was happening."

The office was silent. Cincinnatus' pen made a circle, put a box in it, put a circle inside the box.

"It was a wipeout," Carmody said. "All the officers I'd dealt with were dead. Lopez-Montezuma was going to be executed. There was nobody to give the money to. There wasn't even an army."

"What are you going to do when they catch up with you?" Cincinnatus inquired.

"There's nobody to catch up. What do you want me to do—leave the money on some peon's doorstep?"

Scratching his head, Cincinnatus rumbled, "I'll admit it's without precedent. I might do an opinion on this," he speculated.

"If anybody wants my opinion," Laura volunteered, "I'd say he should put it all in the bank and wait a year."

Tom laughed. Out of his disappointment was coming a strong counterforce. He thought a moment and said suddenly, "Judge, I'll show you what I'm going to do. Open the safe."

Cincinnatus produced the money-belt he had left the night before. "There's a thousand dollars here," Tom said. "I'm going to need five times the cattle I've got to stock Snacktrack. Somebody's going to be glad to sell some heifers and long-two's and not have to bother shipping them. I'll pick up what I can and move them out to my old place. After we tie Tig up, I'll move them along."

The heel of Cincinnatus' hand angrily struck the desk. "And what if we don't tie him up? What if this found money of yours disappears? My God, Tom, you could cover all the land you've got now with a couple of saddle-blankets! And you want to buy another thousand dollars' worth of cattle!"

Tom said patiently, his eyes still glinting with excitement, "If Cornelius, or anybody else, thinks I can be bluffed out, this ought to show him!"

"And if your money doesn't come through for a few weeks, it ought to show you," Laura exclaimed.

Tom grinned, a rashness coming up in him. "Maybe I'll kidnap Tig and take him out with me, Papoose. I'm going out this morning to see what Snaketrack needs before the snow flies."

Cincinnatus was watching with disapproval. "Be sure it's snow that flies, Tom—not lead. Listen, boy! I'm going to tell you something . . ."

"No, Judge," Tom interrupted. "Everybody's told me something. But all I know is that I made this money myself. And I did it without advice. From here on out, I'll get along just about that way."

Cincinnatus turned to his desk. "All right, Tom. Try it your way. If it doesn't work, I hope you'll still be able to try mine."

In the parlor, as she helped Tom on with his coat, Laura was cold. "Did you have to hurt him to make him understand you aren't taking his advice any more?"

The lightness, the eagerness, was growing in him. He thought of the gold-and-lavender basin called Snaketrack. . . of the chocolate-brown shapes of his cattle on the range. He took her elbows and said, "I'll always take his legal advice, Laura. But I'll plan my own fight strategy. I know where I'm going, and I'm going there fast."

Her chin was up. She looked very young, very sweet, but one of the things she had learned during his year away was haughtiness. She could take all the warmth out of her face and leave it as cold as winter sunlight. That same obscure maleness in him was touched with resentment.

In the judge's office, the clock whirred and bonged twice. Laura said coolly, "I'll have to hurry, Tom. Mike's taking me shopping."

"Will you do something for me?" Tom asked.

She studied him. "What?"

Tom leaned over and kissed her. But it was he who was startled. She made such a convincing show of coolness that it was surprising to find her lips so warm. It was surprising, and then breath-taking, and Tom's hands tightened on her arms and he held Laura until she suddenly turned her head away. They faced each other silently, the girl rubbing her arms in hurt and astonishment, Tom standing awkwardly.

"Is—is that what you wanted me to do for you?" Laura asked calmly.

"No," Tom said, and he had to reach back to the glib remark he had been going to make: *Tell Ridge it doesn't tickle when I kiss you.* "No," he said, "it doesn't matter. It was just a joke, but—I'm sorry."

"I'm sorry too, Tom. It was hardly fair to Mike, or to me, was it?"

He felt ungainly, red-faced, but he could not forget how her lips had felt; the soft impression was still on his mouth. He wanted to reach up and touch it. But then he grinned, unexpectedly, and said:

"It was just one of those fool things a man does when

51

he's been in Mexico too long. I'll make a note of it: Don't kiss Laura unless she asks you to."

And when he went back down the stairs, he knew something: it was going to hurt when Laura married Ridge. He had accepted her and Judge Cincinnatus so long that it seemed to him he held a mortgage on the affections of both. There would be something sad about that bright little parlor when Laura was gone.

—8—

THE DAY WAS half-spent when Carmody left the judge's office. Standing in the bleached sunlight, he gazed up the road past the bank, past the coal-yard and Brown's Carriage Works, to a line of wintry poplars running at right angles to the main street and margining the country road. The road turned south to Bannerman's big Cross Anchor ranch and the dime-sized spread Tom had tried to ranch, the grassy basin called Snaketrack.

He thought of his camp on Crooked River, of chopping wood on clear amber mornings—of the giant stillness of the nights. And suddenly he knew that he needed nothing so much as to get out of town. He needed to see his own land again, to ride this land he was going to ranch. It seemed to him that all the things that complicated a man's life happened in buildings. He would be glad to be out of sight of them.

He remembered his joking threat to kidnap Tignal Jones until the lease money should come up from El Paso; to take him out of Holt Bannerman's reach. He could not do that. But he could ride out to Snaketrack and inspect it for winter needs. He could get his Shorthorns started south, ready to put on the land the day the lease was signed.

He had promised Laura to give Clance Harper a job, and now he looked for him in the saloons and learned from Red Murphy, at the Great Western, that he had gone down to the railroad station. He found him there on a corral-bar, gloomily watching stock being loaded. Tom smoked a cigarette with him. Then he asked:

53

"How'd you like to work for me, Clance? I'm hiring."

"You know I'm fifty years old, don't you?" Harper grunted. "May go rheumatic on you, or come down with the weak trembles. You don't want to run a risk like that."

"I know you were twice the judge of livestock Bannerman ever was," Tom said. "He'd always run you down as a cowprod, but just the same he'd give you a blank check and send you to a pure-bred ranch to buy his bulls when he was too busy to go himself. I could use a talent like that, myself."

"How's that?"

"I'm going to be understocked when I move onto Tig Jones' ranch. I've got a thousand cash to spend on cattle. Want to pick out some cattle for me today?"

Harper thought about it, and said, "Why not? I ought to be able to pick up a few right here."

"Have them delivered to my old place," Tom told him. "And find me another rider who isn't too proud to dig post-holes. Send him up to the mesa to help Creed Davis with my Shorthorns. Then get a wagon-load of food and drive it out. . . . It's too bad you burned that hay, Clance. Could have used it."

Harper smiled dreamily. "Tom, I had more fun burning that hay than I've had in twenty years. It was worth it."

At Ribera's Mercantile, Carmody stocked a few staples and loaded them onto a pack-mule. He mounted, but he had only ridden a short distance when he saw a horseman leave the livery stable with a brisk chop of hoofs, a large man with dark hair growing low on his neck. His shoulders were thick and his thighs heavy, and when he glanced across the street and saw Tom waiting there his face was blank, at first, and then tight with watchfulness.

Tom did not take his eyes off Morgan Wiley. He felt the kind of crazy bounce a man feels when he has bet his winter's wages on a single hand of poker. He thought of the fine sarcasm Wiley had used at the station, when he turned Tom's cattle into the freezing rain, and he thought of the three dead cows on the riverbank.

"You're a hard man to find, Morg," he said, and Wiley's face flashed with the savage love of violence he had shown last night. But Tom observed something: Wiley glanced aside at the big door of the livery barn. And he looked at another man standing before the saloon, before he brought his gaze back to Tom.

"You see me now, don't you?" he said.

"And I see your aces in the hole," Tom said. "Why should I make it easy for you? I'll take you on when this isn't Cross Anchor Town any more."

Wiley's mouth turned to irony. "Don't wait too long, Tom. You may get over bein' mad."

Tom said, "That'd be a long time."

Another horseman came from the barn. It was Holt Bannerman. He regarded them with frowning astonishment. He wore a heavy sheepskin coat with his Colt belted over the outside of it. His face looked blunt and emotionless, but abruptly he said to Wiley, "Get up there and help Jim Shaniko. Do you hear me?"

Wiley touched his hat to Tom in insolent salute, and rode off. Bannerman after a moment looked away from Tom and rode after him.

. . . Some headlong emotion in Tom ceased to vibrate. He had never come so close to fighting with a man before without going through with it. And yet he was glad he had avoided it; it was something to look forward to, a ripening apple to pick. If he had picked it today, he would have been taking on half the town.

The day was wearing into long shadows and increasing cold. As he rode up the street, he saw Marshal Mike Ridge crossing to the Cincinnatus apartment. He watched the tall, straight figure for an instant, and then glanced upward. At a window, Laura waved briefly at Ridge and vanished. *I must hurry*, she had said. *Mike's taking me shopping*. It sounded warm and domestic.

Ridge, glancing down the road, saw him and raised his hand. He stood in the cold sunlight waiting for him. "Where to, Tom?" he asked. "Snaketrack?"

"Might be."

"Better not be," said Ridge pleasantly, and he smoothed his tawny mustache with a double-stroke of his cuff. The gesture was coming to infuriate Tom. In it he saw the mannerism of the lawman who fancied himself a fighting marshal. But if Ridge had kept the peace all these years, it was through always being on the side of the winner.

"Have you been talking to Cincinnatus?" Tom asked.

"I've been talking to Cornelius. It's no-go on the money for a while, he says. That means it's no-go on Snaketrack. You ain't planning to put any cattle on it, are you?"

"Not unless I have to."

"What would make you?"

"Other men looking like they meant to."

He raised the reins, but Ridge put up a hand. "If you aren't interested in advice, Tom, I'll bet you're interested in this. Ruth's coming back!"

Despite himself, Tom betrayed his surprise. He almost dropped the lead-rope; then he took a hitch in it and moved on the saddle. "When?"

"Today. Bannerman had a wire."

He was aware of the marshal's steady gaze. He heard him ask curiously, "Anything left between you two?"

"I don't know," Tom said.

"I was hoping there wasn't. Because if you want to know what trouble is—take up with Ruth again."

"Man needs a woman, Mike," Tom smiled.

Ridge said seriously, "He does. Even a man like Bannerman. Ruth was just about everything to him after his wife died. This last year's been pure hell for him. Think of what he's feeling now. The prodigal daughter returned! If you were to step up and take her away from him again—"

"Love's a pretty important thing," Tom said seriously.

Ridge stepped back to the walk. "Not half so important as staying alive," he said mildly. Then he added, "If you're out near the Agency, keep your eye peeled for Chunk McAllister. He was in some scrape or other. A boy came in after the judge a while ago. It's out of my bailiwick, but it wouldn't hurt you to watch out for him, since you and him tangled last night. He's even crazier drunk than he is sober."

—9—

I⊤ WAS A three-hour ride from Soledad to Tom's old headquarters on Crooked River. Near dusk, he reached the turnoff at the crest of Johnson Hill. Ahead, and to the left, the country eased off into grassy *vegas*. Tom's hilly ten sections were in the broken rubble of mountains to his right. He sat looking up at it. How could even a cowpuncher in love have imagined he could make out in country like that?

The mountains ran like a blue stone fence from north to south. Crooked River made up in the forested foothills and ran deviously due east. North of the river it was all Cross Anchor, all Bannerman. South of it, below the palisades, was Tignal Jones' ranch. So that Tom's land, wedged against the mountains, was merely a notch in the sweep of range, a gap in the fence, a lost keystone.

He took the cutoff and rode on along the lonely, weed-grown side road. He remembered a man who thought he loved a girl, a girl who thought she loved a man, riding this trail toward a cabin they would come back to after their honeymoon. He could think of them as two people he had known, had pity for, but no connection with. They were a dead Tom Carmody, a forgotten Ruth Bannerman.

Now that the shock of Ridge's news had passed, he could look at the memory of her without emotion. And in a way it was sad—it was like the Mexican coins still in his pocket. They would all be gone, soon, faded forever, and there was a sigh in the thought that a girl who had made such a change in his life could now mean so little.

57

Farther up, the foothills acquired more timber. There were little parks of rich grass, pleasant in summer, snow-choked in winter. Sunset began. The low clouds caught fire, and Tom stopped on a windy ridge amd looked down on his home place.

Bands of poplar striped the mountainside behind it. Darker groves of spruce and fir went up to marblings of early snow. The cabin and round corral were at the head of a wedge of meadow.

He came down the pine slope and rode up the meadow. The wind came clean and cold off the rimrock, as stimulating as brandy. He wondered what it was that made a man need to ranch just a little more than he needed anything else. It was a rude business without flourishes. The seasons were abrupt—too cold or too hot, too dusty or too muddy. Everything was rough—the fences, the cattle, the barns, the oilcloth on which hungry men put their elbows. But when you were all alone, there was something beautiful, even, about a patched corral or a straight flush on a bunkhouse trunk.

He unsaddled the hired pony, wiped its sweaty back dry and rough-curried it. He was deeply tired, and almost shambled toward the cabin with his blankets and food on his shoulder. The leather latch was broken. All around the porch was the litter of Chunk McAllister's occupancy—a rotten peltry on a frame, old cans and papers. He braced himself for the litter within, and entered.

A man sat at the table in the almost-dark cabin.

Tom stood rigidly while his eyes came into focus. He saw a young Mexican with black eyes set shallowly in a yellowsh-brown Mexican face. A cigarette dangled from his lip. A solitaire deck was in his left hand, a Colt in his right.

He said, "Easy, compadre! Unload your blankets and drop your Colt."

Carmody let the blanket roll down and unbuckled his gunbelt. He looked at Pete Trinidad with wry affection. Trinidad—the railroaded Mexican who aspired to be a gunman.

"I'll sit down, Pete," he said, "if it don't make you nervous. When'd you get out of Mexico?"

58

"Couple of weeks ago. I hid out till I could make it across the river. I been hearing big things about you, Don Tomas. So I rode up to see how much of that money you wanted to cut me in for."

Trinidad threw the cards down but kept the revolver. He walked around the table. A tall man, he was narrow as a hall door, parting his hair in the middle, with a flourish. His ears were pointed like those of a lynx. He wore wine-colored boots, striped gray pants, and a black suit-coat.

"You're wearing two guns now," Carmody observed. "Does that make you twice as dangerous?"

Trinidad waved it off, smiling. "You never was afraid of me, Tom. How come?"

"Why should I be, just because Ridge and Shaniko started calling you a gunman? You can get your gun out fast. But can you hit anything?"

"I hit something in Parral one night. I took this fellow's girl away from him and he spit in my face and called me a gringo-lover."

"A hell of a thing to call a man who left the States because everybody called him a Spik."

Unsmiling, the Mexican said, "They don't call me Spik no more, I think."

"You're a pretty tough hombre now, eh?"

"I don' take nothing no more, Tomas. Not from Shaniko or nobody. No gringo calls me a Spik, and no Mexican calls me a gringo-lover." The gun sparkled as he moved it.

"The trouble with you tough guys," said Tom, "is that you all have one soft spot. The neck. Think it over, Pete. How many people ever called you a Spik? One—Shaniko."

Trinidad sat down at the table. "Any whiskey around here?"

"In my blankets."

"Get it out." Trinidad watched Carmody untie the blanket. "How's my good friend, Shaniko?"

"Fine. He was one of the boys who gave me this eye."

"You take a girl away from him, too?"

Tom grinned. "Did you come back to rob me or kill Shaniko?"

"It don' matter. I get both done. I wish I had a gun that time he tried to buy me a drink after I was pardoned. Cow-thief! You serve two years, you never get over bein' a cow-thief.

"I know." Carmody pulled the cork from the quart bottle. "I'll take a drink first, if you don't care."

Trinidad shrugged. Tom drank a swallow, blew out his cheeks, and carelessly set the bottle on the edge of the table. Immediately it toppled. Swearing, Trinidad lunged forward and caught it. Tom swerved in to catch the Colt by the barrel. His fist smacked the Mexican's jaw and Trinidad fell out of the chair. With a flip, Tom had the gun on him. Lying on his side, Trinidad said bitterly, *"Maldito sea!"*

Carmody smiled. "The other one, too, Pete. Don't upset me."

Trinidad delicately shed the other gun, a bone-handled .45. Tom pulled it over with his toe. He punched the shells out of both guns while Trinidad moved back to sit on the rawhide springs of the cot, staring hotly. Tom strapped on his own gun. He did these things unhurriedly. Then he slid both unloaded guns to the Mexican.

"Put 'em away."

Trinidad grunted. "What the hell kinda fella are you? In Mexico, you tell me I'm no-good bom and fire me. Now you give me back my guns."

"You are a no-good bom, Pete. Money, women, and liquor—they're your trouble. That's why I fired you. You couldn't be trusted to stay with a herd till we delivered it. . . . So you think I've got some money, eh?"

"Sure you've got money. You've got a lot of money. You were lucky. You didn't even have to steal it."

"What makes you think you ought to have it?"

"It's mine as much as yours, ain't it?"

Carmody shook his head. "No. Because I've got it. You know what you need, Pete?"

"Sure. A woman."

"You need a job. A low-down thirty-a-month job."

"With you?"

"With me."

Pulling on the cigarette, Trinidad grinned. "Thirty dollars ain't much to kill a man, Tom. It ain't like you to pay to have a job done, neither. What's the matter—Shaniko got the Indian sign on you?"

"I'm not hiring your gun. I'm hiring your rope—and your rep. Some fellows think you came back here to kill him. One of them will be Shaniko himself. He might as well think so, if it makes him nervous."

Trinidad held the cigarette lightly between two fingers, regarding it. "Another man that thinks I came back to kill Jim Shaniko is me. I've got my spot picked. I'm going to be standing on the porch of the Great Western Hotel, and he's going to be across the street coming out of Brophy's Saloon. And I'm going to shoot him in the belly."

"And then," Tom said, "they'll take you out and hang you."

"First," said Pete, "they've got to catch me."

"You're a fool, Pete. How many people know you're back?"

"Nobody. I just stopped to see you on the way in."

Tom rolled a cigarette, the Colt lying on the table as he frowned over the Durham. "There's one thing nobody ever called you yet, Pete. A liar."

"You going to be the first?"

"The last, I hope. Before I let you out of here, I want your word that you won't make another play for that money. I had the responsibility of it. I risked my neck to return it. You played it fast and loose with every señorita in Chihuahua City while I worked. It's mine, Pete, until Lopez-Montezuma organizes another army. Since he's dead, I don't look for that very soon."

Trinidad's lips curled cynically. "And I get a rope and a running iron."

"You get top pay and the privilege of keeping a brand. If you settle down to one girl and save your money, you can buy yourself a piece of land some day. But you're going to jail for attempted robbery if you don't give me your word that you and that money will never try to get together."

Trinidad sighed. "Well, I never figgered you'd have it

in your pocket, anyway. Sure, Tom. I work for you. Do I have to go to church, too, to hold this job?''

''It wouldn't hurt you to go to confession. Except that it would take all winter to catch up.''

The Mexican chuckled. ''Only thing I don't see, Tom— what for do you want cowpunchers on a spread like this?''

Tom leaned back. ''I'm giving this back to the timber wolves. I'm taking Snaketrack away from Bannerman.''

Trinidad stared, and swore softly. Tom said, ''We're marking time now, until my money comes up from El Paso.''

Trinidad pursed his lips, and when he had blown smoke at the ceiling his lips smiled. ''What if you have to give it back?''

''Dammit,'' Tom said, ''I told you—''

''But I ain't told you, Tom. Lopez-Montezuma ain't dead! He bought his way out of jail before they could execute him. I seen him in El Paso. He looked like he might be looking for somebody.''

The silence in the cabin was complete. Tom sat woodenly. After a moment he got up and lighted the lamp. Then he sat down and stared at the small, caged flame. ''Is that straight?''

Trinidad raised his hand. ''That's straight, Tomas! . . . He know where you come from?''

Tom stirred uncomfortably. ''Yeah. I had to give him my life's history before he'd trust me with cattle-buying money. Yeah, he knows where to find me.''

A frowning sympathy lay in the Mexican's face. ''What you gonna do, Tom? Give it back? That'd finish you here, won't it?''

Tom got up, and set his lips and drew his arm back with the cigarette. Then he hurled it out the door and stared after it. He was breathing fast. He said, ''Yes. That would finish me.''

—10—

THE CABIN WAS not a tight one. It was the sort of structure—
mud-chinked, green-logged—that a man built when he was
fired in July and had until November to raise four walls
and a roof. The wind hissed between the cracked chinks
that night and in the morning it took an hour to melt the
chill from the room.

They boiled Arbuckle and fried salt pork and potatoes.
They sat at the limber-legged table, the American and the
Mexican. They talked about the revolution, and Tom said:

"You're sure Lopez-Montezuma got away, eh?"

"Seguro que sí! Diaz put up fifty thousand pesos reward
for him."

Tom stirred sandy sugar into his coffee. "Well, I'm
glad for the little guy. He's all right. He'd do everything
for the peons that Diaz wouldn't. A little land. A shack of
their own."

"But he ain't going to do you much good, eh?"

"Not one damn bit," Tom said.

He went to stand in the doorway, looking out on a
hillside ablaze with golden aspen. He found his thoughts
swinging to Judge Cincinnatus, and he wondered, *Will he
help me out of this, if there's a way out? He'd a helped
me quicker*, he decided, *if I hadn't cut his knees from
under him yesterday.*

He looked around at Trinidad, who was sluicing the tin
dishes in a pan of hot water. "Did you really think you
could get any of that money out of me, Pete?"

The Mexican grinned. "Well, I figgered it was worth

63

trying. If I didn't get it, the general would. I wouldn't 'a' shot you, Tom. Just creased you a little. . . . What you gonna do now?"

"Act like I owned the place," Tom said. "Maybe I can work out a dicker with him."

"I'll tell you the only dicker I'd be interested in, if I was Lopez-Montezuma: cash on the line."

"Maybe I can even rustle that."

"Hell, you must be twenty thousand in the hole already!"

"Just about," Tom said.

They loafed about the cabin half the morning, and suddenly Tom remembered the last thing Marshal Ridge had told him. There had been trouble at the Agency, and Cincinnatus was going out. If he could catch him, he could talk this out right now. He felt a quick lift, and going to the rawhide *aparejo* hanging from the ceiling, out of the way of pack-rats, he took out a can of sardines and some hardtack.

"Pete," he said, "I'm going to see my lawyer. He ought to be passing the old stage station about noon. How's about you going up to Mesa Roja and helping Clance Harper and the other boys I've hired with the Shorthorns?"

"Sure. Clance know what to do with them?"

Tom could see them, in his mind's eye—the Shorthorns . . . the cattle Harper had bought yesterday and today . . . the mavericks he would be bringing home from the Agency one day soon—he saw these five hundred and more cattle crowded onto ten sections not fit for fifty.

"We'll hold them here a few days, I reckon," he told Trinidad.

"And by that time," Trinidad told him, "it's going to look like sheep had pastured here all winter. Well, *buena suerte,* Tom. I say one thing—you got a helluva lot of guts!"

The foothills sloughed off to a rolling mesa which ended at a five-mile palisade, falling precipitously a thousand feet to a basin yellow-brown with autumn grasses. Crooked River came around at Tom's right, brawling through the hills, and followed a timbered gorge to trace the foot of the palisade. Sitting his pony on the rim of the palisade, Tom looked down on this land he had thought was his. It had never looked much farther away when he was a green rancher with forty dollars hidden in a baking-powder can under his hearth. But he could still yearn over the rich lowlands running south and east, rich with hard-cured grama. Near the river, he made out the half-healed scars where a younger, more energetic Tig Jones had long ago raised hay to coax a few more cows through the winter.

It made him think of the hay ranch Clance Harper had operated this year—Bannerman's old homestead place. He rolled a cigarette while he waited for the judge to come along, gazing down the river. The hay ranch lay on the north bank of the stream between the bosque and the palisades, a quarter-section strip. He could see it plainly, the hayed area yellow, the old fruit orchard a violet tangle of branches. Here and there in the fields he discerned black stains where Clance had burned his hay.

He saw no rider on the palisade trail. By this he assumed that the judge had not yet passed on his way to the Apache reservation, ten miles southeast. Tom had finished two cigarettes when he heard a rider in the small timber behind him. Because caution had come to be a part of him in Mexico, he walked into a scope of piñons and waited. Soon a horse came into view on the road, and he stared a moment, then smiled to himself and walked forward.

Laura had halted her pony by his own and was looking about for him. She wore a split doeskin skirt and a dark jacket, and her hair was in black pigtails coming forward over her shoulders. She rode a side-saddle with a short buggy-gun in a scabbard.

She saw Tom, and at once her expression was relieved. When he reached her and put his hands up, she let him swing her to the road. She was a light and fragile burden. Tom released her reluctantly.

"Thank heaven!" she said. "I came by your cabin, but there was no one there. I couldn't tell from the tracks whether you'd gone back to town or come on, and I didn't have time to go back." She looked at him in sincere gladness. "Tom. I've never been so glad to see anyone."

"But yesterday you'd never been so glad to see anyone go. When do I believe you?"

She smiled, yet faintly, her eyes serious. "Dad's gone after Chunk McAllister," she said.

She walked a few steps along the rim, easing out the stiffness of the ride.

"What about it?" Tom said. "He can handle Chunk. He's the only one who ever could."

"He always could, before. But Chunk's—gone bad, Tom."

Tom thought of the wolf-hunter before the saloon that night, cursing the men who would not buy him a drink, and how Chunk had turned on him at the railroad station with Tom's whiskey still hot in him.

"What's he done?" he asked.

With obvious hesitation, she turned to look out over the wide, whispering basin.

"It was over one of the squaws at the Agency. He got drunk and almost killed the girl's father with a knife. Then he—forced himself on the girl. One of the boys came in to tell Dad. All Dad told me was that there was a little something he had to straighten out. But he left in such a hurry that I got suspicious. I looked in the Agency journal he keeps and found out what had happened."

"Why didn't you tell Ridge?"

"I did." She turned back to the horses. Tom detected a stiffness in her. "He said he could lose his job if he meddled in Agency matters, and anyway Dad was able to handle it. But I'm not sure, with Chunk in real trouble. Dad was going to talk to the girl last night and go on up this morning."

Tom took up the reins of her horse and helped her onto the saddle. He looked into her face and saw the fear there, and what he had been about to say was what he did not say at all. He told her, "Ridge is right, Laura. The judge can handle Chunk, drunk or sober. But let's try to catch him, anyway."

They started down the trail criss-crossing the face of the palisade. What Tom was wondering was how Chunk McAllister, who ordinarily had not the price of a drink, had contrived to take back an unopened quart or two with him. If a man looked closely enough, he might make out Bannerman's fine hand in this. Bannerman, wanting a day or two alone with Tignal Jones, might regard this as a fair means of siphoning the judge out of town. . . .

They reached the bottom, passed Clance Harper's hay ranch, and crossed the river at the old ford. On the other side were the derelict remains of an old stage station, the shakes askew on the roof, the hitch-rack sagging like a string. Farther down the river, Apache Hills ran transversely across the basin. East of the hills was the Apache reservation. In one of the dry canyons of the hills was Chunk McAllister's cabin.

Down here it was warm, a thousand feet lower than the highlands. There was still some green along the river, a few leaves on the cottonwoods. They rode briskly, working toward the hills. They were close enough now to see the bars of tan rimrock through the timber. Tom saw him, then, coming down the trail which crossed the Apache Hills from the Agency side. Discovering them, too, Cincinnatus pulled up to wait. In about twenty minutes they reached him.

Cincinnatus was grizzled, bespectacled and truculent. He wore no hat, and his scalp shone under the badger-gray hair. He was carrying only a Colt, Tom saw. He stared fiercely at Laura.

"Laura, what in the devil are you doing out here?" he demanded.

Laura regarded him coolly. "Why didn't you tell me what you were planning to do?"

"I did! That fool Charlie One-Bear has been making *tiswin* again. Boy came in to tell me. If I hadn't come along when I did, he'd have had the whole reservation drunk." He peered up a shallow canyon opened ahead. "I thought I might as well take a look at the shoring around Iron Pipe spring while I was out here."

Laura regarded him quietly. "You're going to try to take Chunk McAllister back, aren't you? I looked in your journal."

Color struck through the lawyer's face. "When did I

start governing my life by female opinions? Yes, I'm after Chunk. The Indians say he's holed up at the spring. By God, he's gone too far! He's on his way to a government pokey this time. If you two want to wait here, you'll see me come back in an hour with a halter around his neck.''

Tom shook his head. "He's gone bad, Judge. He won't take anything even from you.''

"Drunk or sober, sane or crazy, I know every bone in McAllister's head. If you want to watch, all right. But you'll have to stay out of sight when I go to work on him.''

He rode ahead, but Laura spurred up beside him. "Dad, the only way to handle him now is with a forked stick, like a rattlesnake. Let Tom help you.''

"I've dealt with criminals for the last forty years, Laura. When I need help, I'll retire.''

Laura glanced back at Tom, a shine of tears in her eyes. Tom winked as the judge rode on. "We'll skin this cat another way, if his way doesn't work out,'' he told her.

They followed hillside trails for twenty minutes, coming finally through a low pass into a meadow yellow with dead grasses. Cincinnatus rode more slowly, his eyes keen, his nose out like that of a sniffing hound. Suddenly he pulled in sharply and hauled his horse across the trail.

"Yonder!'' he said.

Carmody leaned on the swell of his saddle, squinting through a screen of aspen at a small log cabin lying at the base of a hill. A feather of smoke rose from the chimney. A man on the porch moved quickly and Carmody caught a shine of metal.

Cincinnatus spoke harshly. "You two stay here. The only way to handle him is to bluff him down.''

"Lunatics don't bluff,'' Tom declared. "Give me twenty minutes to work around behind the cabin. He'll come out if we both hit him at once.''

"I know that fool, Tom. I know his strong points and his weak ones. Coyotin' is the best thing he does. Standing up to a bluff is the worst.''

He touched spurs to his pony and jogged ahead.

Suddenly Laura gripped Tom's arm. "Stop him, Tom!''

"Leave him alone," Tom grunted. "Maybe he knows what he's doing."

. . . In the meadow, Cincinnatus halted. "Chunk!" he called.

From inside the cabin, McAllister's voice sounded muffled. "Turn that hoss around, Jedge!"

"Don't be silly," Cincinnatus snapped. "I'm not here to punish you. I'm taking you in, so that you can tell us why you did it."

Carmody could see the figure in the door. A pulse in him beat strongly. He could hear Laura's rapid breathing.

"Nobody ain't taking me in!" Chunk stated. "I'll ram this slug right a-down your gullet, Jedge. Them Injuns cain't tell nothing but lies."

"That's what we want to find out, the truth. Put the gun down," Cincinnatus said flatly. "We're going back."

He walked the horse in, his hand clear of his Colt. The bounty hunter slipped out of sight in the cabin. Suddenly Tom thrust Laura aside and leaned against a rock, pulling a slow aim on the doorway. He saw the lustre of McAllister's rifle against the dust of shadows. And now Chunk shouted again, a furious eagerness packed into his voice.

"No demnition squaw-man is taking me anywheres, Jedge! Pass that travoy, and you git it."

An Indian drag-cart lay in the yard. Cincinnatus reined in beside it. He stared at the cabin. Then he stiffly threw his leg over the cantle and dismounted. Staring at the cabin, he adjusted his spectacles. With an angry gesture of his hand, he walked forward.

. . . In the doorway, smoke blossomed like an ugly flower. The shot tore the silence.

Laura's scream was knifelike in Tom's ears. He was on the point of firing when the judge staggered into his line of fire. Laura loped her pony back from the rocks. Tom swore and swerved aside and took a snap-shot at the cabin. Laura's horse reared with the gunshot.

Running forward, Tom caught the bridle. He dragged Laura out of her saddle and thrust her against the ground behind a stump at the clearing's edge. Kneeling beside her, he levered up another shell, while Cincinnatus sat

69

down heavily like a man too weary to go farther. The judge sat with his head bent forward. Then he lay over on his side.

On the porch, the heavy smut of black-powder drifted away. A moment later hoofs struck the stony earth behind the cabin. Tom ran for the trail to the hillside. A sorrel horse was cutting through the small timber, angling for a low ridge. For a moment it pulled in, and Tom instinctively plowed into a gather of rocks, falling as he went. There was a slog of heavy-caliber fire. The ball exploded in the rocks with a puff of granite dust. Tom threw the gun barrel up and got the sorrel hide of the horse under his sights. The horse moved as he fired. He heard the bullet strike a tree. McAllister was slashing deep into the junipers.

Tom fired twice more before he lost sight of the hunter. Then he ran back to the judge. Laura was on her knees beside him. Tom stood over them. He saw the lawyer's eyes come up to him. His spectacles lay broken beside him. His coat was torn at the shoulder and blood was spreading from a wound. His face was pale as a candle, but he smiled waxily.

"If it please your Honor," he whispered. "I move the court adjourn."

—11—

THEY STAYED THAT night in Chunk McAllister's cabin at Iron Pipe spring. With sweet oil and bluestone he found in a cupboard, Tom dressed the judge's wound. The bullet had torn raggedly through the large muscle of Cincinnatus' shoulder. Laura ripped cloth from a petticoat to make a bandage. By morning the bleeding had stopped, but the judge was still in pain, weak and feverish. "Can you ride?" Tom asked him.

"I can do anything I have to," Cincinnatus stated. "This would be a hell of a place to convalesce. I'd get the screwworms in this wound sure as hell."

So in midmorning they left the cabin, riding slowly, to the stage station on the bank of Crooked River, resting here an hour before crossing the stream. The road led upward through thickets toward Clance Harper's hay ranch.

Cincinnatus was watching Tom. "You ain't talked much, Tom!"

"I've thought a little."

"About Chunk, or Bannerman?"

"When you think about one, you think about the other."

"That ain't true, Tom! This was Chunk's party. It'd been due."

"Due, yes—but who supplied the liquor? He was cadging drinks when I saw him in the Great Western the other night. But when he left town, he had a quart with him. There was a new empty in the cabin. Who bought it for him?"

"Tom," Cincinnatus sighed, "justice has been my trade.

71

I've found that by and large, when a man wants somebody killed, he goes about it pretty direct. Is there anything direct about getting a lunatic drunk so he'll ravish an Indian girl—so I'll have to go out and corral him?''

"Is there anything direct about Bannerman?" Tom countered. "He wanted you out of town while he worked on Tig. And the quickest way to get you out was through trouble on the Agency. What would make trouble any quicker than Chunk and a quart of whiskey?''

"Well—nothing. But that's pretty involved chess you're playing. And here's something else you don't seem to realize: Bannerman's no killer. He's hard, but—he's no killer.''

"Up to now, he hasn't needed to kill," Tom contended. "Except once. Did you know he started for my place with a rifle after Ruth ran off?''

"No, but it don't make him a killer. The only thing he'd kill over is Ruth. Every man's got something he'd kill over. . . . What would you kill over, Tom?''

Staring ahead, Tom said, "I'd damn near kill over you, Judge. If Chunk'd killed you, I'd be in the hills right now, and I wouldn't be back till I'd dropped him. And then I'd go after Bannerman.''

"Tom, Tom!" Cincinnatus said.

"Tom's still ambitious to be a gunman," Laura told him.

Cincinnatus did not speak for so long that Tom glanced at him. The judge's face was thoughtful, his eyes almost dreamy. Finally he said, "If you're looking for a killer, look at Wiley. There's your pattern. If Wiley needed to, he'd kill.''

" Sure," Tom said, "but he learned it from Bannerman.''

Cincinnatus smiled in a tired fashion and shook his head.

Beyond a tangle of ironwood they came within view of Harper's hay ranch, the field stubbled gold, the orchard a haze of gray. Laura spoke decisively. "We'll stay the night here, Dad. You're white as a sheet.''

"All right, Laurie," the judge sighed. "For once I'm too weak to argue it.''

As they rode across the field, Laura said suddenly, "Isn't there someone at the house?"

Tom looked and saw a yellow buggy gleaming in the mid-afternoon sunlight before the unpainted two-story house. "Looks like Bannerman's turnout," Cincinnatus declared.

"Yes, I think it is," Laura said.

She looked quickly at Tom, then. He had not said anything, but he had recognized the buggy from the first. His face had not changed, except to lighten, but he lifted the reins without warning and rattled his spurs against the horse's flanks. Laura called his name, but he rode on at an easy lope toward the cabin, straight in the saddle.

Before he reached the yard, he saw Bannerman come out of the house. The rancher stood with one hand on the porch-rail, square-set and watchful. Here, where he had got his start as a rancher, where Ruth had been born, where he had scraped up the money for his first grazing lease, he looked out-of-place now. He looked like a too-large tree in a too-small yard. You need humbling, Tom thought. And maybe this is the time to start it.

As Tom dismounted, Bannerman came down the steps. His face was brown and hard as wood, cut with harsh lines. Yet he did not look in any way threatening, but puzzled. Tom started toward him, but stopped with his hands hanging.

He was looking at someone who had just come onto the porch—a girl. She was blonde, composed, and neat in a dark-gray gown and a short blue cape. She looked steadily at him, searching his face; and after a moment she smiled and said:

"You look terribly fierce, Tom. I thought you'd be glad to see me."

Tom raised a hand and awkwardly tipped his hat. "Hello, Ruth," he said. "I—I heard you were coming."

She came forward, smiling. But her father changed his position so that he blocked the steps. With a set mouth, he stared at Tom.

"What's the matter out there?" he demanded. "Is that Cincinnatus? He rides like he's hurt."

"You didn't know about it? Chunk McAllister shot him last night."

Bannerman received the news without expression. "*Shot him?*"

"He was drunk," Tom said patiently. "Somebody'd sent him out to the Agency with a bottle of whiskey. I thought you'd know about that."

Bannerman took his glance away and strode to the buggy. He mounted, shook the lines from the whipstock and drove down the road to meet the judge and Laura.

Tom and Ruth stood facing each other.

After a moment she laughed. "I really didn't mean to frighten you, Tom."

He could feel the color in his face. "You did, though. . . . We came back about the same time, didn't we? I wonder what Morg thinks about it?"

"He's a little curious," the girl admitted, and then she laughed again, softly, as if from gladness that wanted to be expressed. "Tom, the things I've been hearing about you!"

"Small towns have to talk," he said.

He had carried a picture of a thin girl with an immature prettiness. He wondered where he had got it. For, looking at her, he realized she had changed little, yet the prettiness was a real beauty, her eyes were cool and candid, her skin fair and perfectly clear. He looked at the deep lower lip and remembered the yielding softness of it. . . .

"Small towns and big ranchers," she commented.

"Where were you?" he asked.

"With my aunt in California. I wouldn't let her tell him I was there. It's done him good, I think. He's given me his old homestead place as a coming-home present!"

Tom thought of old Clance Harper, bringing the place from a thicket back to productivity. He wondered if she knew, and he wondered again whether it would matter to her.

". . . Married?" he asked her.

"So soon after our big affair? Of course not."

She looked at him in a grave, searching way. Standing so close, Tom had the sensation that they had been part of something secret and exciting. For a while they had been more to each other than anyone in the world. But all that was left of it now was a remote tingle.

"You didn't get my letter?" Ruth asked him.

"Yes." He gazed down the road, where Bannerman was helping the judge into the buggy. It was hard to say, but Tom told her frowningly, "It wouldn't help to try it again, Ruth. It's gone, whatever it was. I'm sure of it, if there's nothing else I am sure of."

"How can you be sure?" She said it quickly, impatiently, and then, after a moment, "Some day, you know, I'm going to own all this land. Wouldn't it serve him right if your cattle were pastured on it then?"

The remark was less startling because of its implications than for the cool, smiling way in which she delivered it. Without taking his glance from her, he began to nod. "Almost anything would serve him right, after yesterday."

"What do you mean by that?"

"Stick around," Tom said. "You'll pick it up."

Her eyes were peremptory. "Tom, what's the matter?"

He went up on the porch and glanced into the cabin. Harper had refurbished the parlor with rough furniture, a table and chair and cot. There were blankets on the cot and plenty of stove wood. He turned back and saw the buggy roll into the yard. It occurred to him that although Ruth knew Judge Cincinnatus had been shot, she had not asked one question about him.

When he saw Bannerman helping the judge down, the diffused anger he had carried for twenty-four hours came into sudden, sharp focus. All at once he knew what he was going to do to show Bannerman how the game was played in Union County.

They made Cincinnatus comfortable on the cot and Tom built a fire. Laura hung a kettle on a crane, while Ruth talked to the judge. Bannerman asked questions about Chunk McAllister. Once Tom heard him say, "Judge, I'm damned sorry. I want you to understand that—even though Chunk was on my payroll . . ."

"I understand," Cincinnatus said coolly. "You know what I think? I think it's damned fine Clance Harper fixed this house up for us. Who'd have thought I'd have been needing it?''

Bannerman went onto the porch to smoke. Tom made sure there was nothing more he could do. He told Laura he would send Doctor Brough out when he reached town. "I don't like leaving you alone," he said, "but I think he ought to have attention."

"Of course," she said, and he saw her eyes flick to Ruth, and then come back. "She's as pretty as ever," she said softly.

"Once upon a time," Tom told her, "that seemed to matter."

He went out into the early dusk. He walked to his pony and adjusted the latigo, and swung up. As he rode past the house, Bannerman came forward.

"Get it out of your head," he stated, "that I had anything to do with this."

"I wish I could prove half the things I think about you," Tom said.

"Since you can't," Bannerman said, "what do you plan to do?"

"Move onto Snaketrack," Tom told him. "Put every cow I've got onto Snaketrack, as soon as I can move them. I'm going in tonight and get started."

Bannerman's hand lifted the cigar to his mouth. He drew on it and the cigar glowed gray-red, and he said:

"If you take your cows in there, Carmody, you'll never take them out alive. So help me God."

—12—

IT WAS PAST EIGHT when Tom Carmody rode into Soledad. Lights from store-fronts glittered on the rind of frost in the street. There was a witch-hazel sting to the dry highland air. Riding down a side-street toward Doctor Brough's home, he felt his weariness. A shadowy pack of worries stalked him. He regarded them soberly, for there was not one he knew how he was going to handle.

Three days ago, he had been in a fury with Phil Cornelius because he would not honor his check to Tig Jones until Tom's money came up from El Paso. Now there was a threat over the money greater than Cornelius had provided, the shadow of a man who had cheated a firing squad. If Cornelius should announce tomorrow that the funds had come up from El Paso, Tom did not know whether he would dare use them or not. And how long could he stall Tig Jones, who was anxious to leave town, and would know the money was ready? In an agony of frustration, Tom struck the saddlehorn. It was not stolen; it was found money. But what if Lopez-Montezuma, bearded little general of the peasant armies, was ready to march again? Thirty thousand dollars would buy a lot of tortillas and gunpowder. And perhaps it could be argued that his new army was son and heir to the old one?

As he had done before, Tom thought, *The judge will come up with something!*

But if he did, it would be no thanks to Bannerman, who was no less guilty of the attack on Cincinnatus for having employed a drunken lunatic instead of a Colt. Chunk

77

McAllister had pulled the trigger, but Bannerman had loaded the gun. It was a complex and exasperating pattern; but it came back to one factor you could almost overlook in the confusion:

Snaketrack.

Tom saw that his threat to put his cattle on Snaketrack was the one clear-cut thing he could do, now. It went past maneuvering. When Cincinnatus fell with a bullet through his shoulder, a door had been opened, and Tom had seen exactly how far Bannerman was willing to go to keep Snaketrack. He could not complain, now, if Tom followed his lead.

But in a corner of his mind he saw himself trying to justify his action to the judge himself, and he heard Cincinnatus saying again, *He's hard . . . but he's no killer.* You're wrong! Judge, Tom thought grimly. The first thing you've got to know about Bannerman is that killing isn't past him. He'd kill over Ruth, and he'd kill over Snaketrack.

Tom knew and believed this, and tomorrow he would set in motion a plan that was based on it. Get Snaketrack. Hold it. And then square it with Lopez-Montezuma however he could, if the general ever showed up.

He saw the doctor whirl off in his box buggy, and went back to town and called at Marshal Ridge's office. Ridge "bached" in a room off the jail; he came out thumbing suspenders over his underwear. Seeing Tom, his face at once slackened in surprise.

"Tom!" he said. And then, "You haven't tangled with Bannerman?"

"Seems to be on everybody's mind, Mike. No, this is over Chunk McAllister. He shot Cincinnatus yesterday afternoon."

Ridge's hand found a chair and he sat down, staring at Tom. Then he put a hand to his forehead and Tom saw the nails whiten. "I knew—as sure as God, I knew something! . . ."

"Why didn't you go out after him, then?" Tom asked.

The marshal's face came up angrily. "And don't be giving me any of *that!*" he said. "Except for hot-headed fools like you, I could have gone out, even though the reservation is out of my territory. With you and Wiley sharpening your claws, how's a man going to leave his office for two days?'' His fist came down on the arm of the chair, then, his face breaking wryly, "Is he dead?''

"No. Hit in the shoulder; not too bad, I guess. We brought him to Harper's place. I sent Brough out.''

"Thank God!" Ridge said. "Thank God!" He went into his sleeping room and came back shrugging into a heavy green shirt. "Give it to me fast.''

Tom told him about the shooting. Ridge opened a drawer of his desk and took out three tarnished deputy's badges. "Going after Chunk tonight?" Tom asked him.

"I can't go any earlier!''

"Why don't you go after the man that wanted Cincinnatus killed? Not afraid of him because he used to be big, are you?''

Something in Tom made him bait the marshal, something that was part jealousy over Laura and part Bannerman and part Tom Carmody. He saw Ridge come toward him angrily, smoothing his yellow mustache with his cuff, and felt Ridge's hand take his arm like a vise.

"I've taken all off you that I aim to, Tom,'' Ridge declared. "I've run this office the best I could. I didn't railroad Trinidad because I wanted to. I didn't let Cincinnatus get shot because I was yellow. If I hear either of those things out of you again, you and I are going to have trouble—barefisted trouble. In your way you're no easier to deal with than Bannerman. You're cocky and hotheaded where he goes slow and easy but just as hard. And a hotheaded man can make as much trouble as a mortally mean one. I'm taking no more off either of you.''

Looking into him, Tom saw a little more of Ridge than he ever had. Ridge might strut like a hand-made Buffalo Bill, but there was a core of toughness in him. He said grudgingly:

"Well, you couldn't have helped with Chunk anyway, so don't let it be on your conscience. As far as Trinidad goes—I guess Pete will take that up with Shaniko, when the time comes. He's back, Mike. He's working for me.''

Ridge took his hand away, his face still dark with rancor. He took his hat from a deer-head on the wall, pulled his coat from a chair. "That's fine," he said. "That's great. What are you trying to put together—a Hole-in-the-Wall Gang? So far you've got an outlaw, a drunk, and a man that's after Bannerman for foreclosing on him. And all of them hate Bannerman from the spurs up."

"Try and find somebody that doesn't."

Tom went to the door, but Ridge said sharply, "Tom—you ain't going to hold this shooting against Bannerman, are you?"

Tom shrugged. "Now that I know how it's played, why shouldn't I try a little of the same? I'll have my first bunch of cattle on Snaketrack by tomorrow night."

Ridge did not raise his voice. He continued to button the frogs of his coat. He said, "If you put one steer on that land before the judge says the lease is signed and sealed, I'll jail you. I'll bring you in in handcuffs and slap you in a cell until the law says I have to let you out. . . . Write that down where you won't lose it. Because that's how it's going to be."

Tom stayed in the hotel that night. He was up at daylight, walking through the tender smokes of morning to a cafe, eating slowly, drawing it out, drinking three cups of coffee and drowning the butts of three cigarettes in the dregs.

This was a day of waiting, and Tom found he had forgotten how to wait.

He made a bad business of it—trying the door of the bank twice that morning before finally the green blinds were rolled up. Then the word from Cornelius—that undertaker of a man, ossified with dignity—was that the money had not come up from El Paso. Tom walked over to Tig's rock shack on the bank of the river. Tig was not there. He had slept, Tom supposed, in the back room of the last saloon he visited the night before, he and his snake-in-a-jug. And Tom felt again the flimsy fabric of the armor he wore. A fortune in money that might evaporate in his fingers. A business deal with a man who had not been quite sober in years.

He was beginning wistfully to wish he had written Cincinnatus for advice before he came up from Mexico.

In midmorning he rode up to Mesa Roja to the roundup camp. Creed and Trinidad were cow-hunting with the two punchers Harper had hired for the drive. Harper was riding herd on a bunch of a hundred and fifty cows.

"I bought fifty-six cows with the money you left," he told Tom. "They're on the way down right now. Be down here tomorrow. You want us to start them south, then?"

"And keep going towards Crooked River," Tom said. "We're putting them on Snaketrack. I'll be along before you cross the river."

"Everything fixed up?" Harper asked.

"No," Tom said, curtly.

Returning, he saw Brough's buggy below the Cincinnatus apartment. He went upstairs quickly. The doctor and Laura were in the kitchen.

"Go into the bedroom," Laura told him. "Maybe you can help us to keep him there. He's better, Tom."

Tom found the judge in bed with a writing board on his knees, in a reek of medicines. He wore a flowered flannel nightgown, and his badger-gray hair was rumpled. He was writing with a crow-quill, and now gave Tom a preoccupied smile.

"Brough gives me six weeks in bed," he said. "I'll bring charges for malpractice if he can't do better than that. Tom," he said, crisply, "I'm doing an opinion for the Supreme Court."

"No change there," Tom said.

"It's on this Mexican-money proposition of yours. I want you to give me the details again. I'd like to make up my own mind about whether or not it's yours."

Tom looked closely at him, but saw no slyness in his eyes. At the same time, as much as he would have welcomed help, he did not want to worry the judge with the Lopez-Montezuma news. He told him the story, and Cincinnatus made notes and asked a few questions.

"Beats me!" he admitted. ". . . I suppose we can say

you're the owner of it until the legal owner comes along, eh?" He laughed, but winced and put his hand to his shoulder.

"The only opinion I'm interested in," Tom reproved him, "is Doc's. And if he says six weeks in bed, six weeks it's going to be."

When he left, the doctor had gone, but Laura was waiting in the parlor. She sat on the sofa among the bright squares of an afghan she was making. She did not look up when Tom stopped before her. Her features were sober. The crocheting needle made its bright dipping motions and the yarn was caught in loops, and still she did not look up.

"Hello!" Tom said.

Her eyes rose. They were large and steady—purple-gray and lovely, but now he saw the anger they harbored. "For the first time since I've known you," she said, "I'm truly angry with you."

He moved the squares and sat beside her. He put his hand on hers and held it. "Ridge told you?"

"Yes, when he went by with the posse. I didn't let Dad know. . . . So you've tried Bannerman and found him guilty."

"Listen, Laura!" Tom said. "You can't win a fight by blocking blows. You only wear yourself out. Bannerman's just swung and missed, and if I don't close with him now I may never get another chance."

"Why not? When your money comes through, will things be any different from what they are now?"

"They might. Things seem to be changing pretty fast."

"And you're making some of the changes yourself, Tom. Mike told me Pete Trinidad is back. Why did you hire him?"

"Because he's a good worker. Anything between him and Shaniko is—between him and Shaniko."

"It won't look that way to Bannerman."

Tom dropped her hand and stood up. "I don't care how it looks!" He felt angry and blocked. He wanted approbation, and he got cross-questioning. She looked at him as coolly as a bank teller asking for references. He had an intense desire to kiss her; he closed his fists and glared at her.

"Laura, I don't see any other way to show him I'm not bluffed. If I let this pass, he'd be on Snaketrack next and dare me to take it away from him."

"I don't think that's true, Tom."

"I can't take a chance that it is. I've got to play it the way I see it, even if Ridge tries to stop me."

He continued to stare at her until she shook her head. "I'm not your conscience, Tom. I haven't asked you not to, have I?"

"It's plain enough that you think I'm wrong, though!"

"I do think you're wrong—but I won't ask any more favors of you."

He picked up his hat, but frowned at her a moment longer. Exasperated, he asked, "What is it about a pretty girl that makes her half-right no matter how wrong she is?"

"I don't know," she smiled. "What is it?" He donned his hat and went to the door, and then she spoke. "I don't know whether you've thought of this, Tom. I hope it's just an oversight."

He frowned. "Well, say it!"

"I mean the effect your—your invasion of Snaketrack will have on Dad. The reason I didn't let him know is that the doctor thought it might upset him dangerously. He's involved in that land as much as you are, you know. He's trustee for it, and it's his job to keep it clear. And of course if you go ahead, he'll know."

Tom took off his Stetson and scratched his head. "Did Doc say that?"

"He said that, at Dad's age, he's lucky to be alive today. And that he'll have to have all the breaks if he's to avoid serious complications. There's a sound in his lung he doesn't like." She began gathering the bright squares of wool. "Beyond that, of course, it's entirely up to you."

Tom went back to her, and taking her by the shoulders gave her a shake. Suddenly he smiled. "Next time say it first, and save me a lot of jawing. You win, Papoose! When it comes to men, you'll always win."

Smiling, Laura stood up, the top of her head coming to his nose. Standing so close, he saw the smooth luster of her lips, the little cleft of her upper lip.

"If I'd lost this time," she smiled, "I'd think that I didn't know much about men."

"The way I see it," Tom told her, "you don't."

"What does that mean?" she demanded. "Bannerman?" But he moved away, crossing the red Indian carpet to the door. He went on to the landing, and spoke from the shadows.

"No, not Bannerman. Tom Carmody."

—13—

AND AGAIN IT was a waiting day, a day with long hours and brittle sunlight, and tension. He saw the Bannerman buggy rattle across the foot of Front Street, and knowing the rancher was back, he wondered why. There were more reasons why Bannerman should be out of town, at his home ranch or at a roundup camp, than in town.

But there was a stronger magnet to pull him here than existed anywhere else. A dissipated, cynical magnet who wore a goatee and carried a jugged rattlesnake under his arm. When Tom thought about Tignal Jones, he was filled with anxiety.

This minute, Tig might be saying to Bannerman, "The hell with waiting for Tom Carmody. Let's see your money—"

Tom walked to the Great Western Hotel, where he had been in the habit of getting his mail. In the small, dank lobby, the elderly clerk turned over to him a stockman's catalogue and a livestock journal. He told Tom that Tig had been looking for him that morning.

"Still lugging that damn rattlesnake around. He took me for another six bits. If the snake don't starve to death pretty soon, I will." He held his hand out, palm up. "I'll be *dogged* if I see why a man can't git it through his head—!"

"So will I," said Tom. "Where would he be now?"

"Might be at the livery stable. Him and Harry Bailey play chess now and ag'in."

"Did he say why he wanted me this morning?"

"No, but he was in a hell-fired rush."

Tom rolled the catalogue and put it under his arm. "If you see him, tell him to go up to Cincinnatus' office and wait there till you find me. . . . What do you hear from the posse?"

"Hell! They're driftin' back already!" said the clerk. "The trail froze out in the mountains."

Tom stood very quietly, thinking about a marshal who could not hold a twenty-four-hour trail. If Ridge had lost it, it was because he wanted to. It made his own promise to Laura to stay off Jones' ranch all the more bitter, and in a slow voice he said, "God damn them, Ike! God damn every cowardly man of them."

He went out and walked to the Great Western, where he bought a quart of whiskey. Up on the mesa the wind would be sharp as a honed knife. Night was coming on. He would carry to Creed and Trinidad and Harper the cheer of the whiskey and the word that they would not be moving to Snaketrack after all. He led the pony across the street to Bailey's Livery, slid the great door aside and went into the warm stable-reek.

Bailey came from his office, a tall, thin man in overalls with a blade-like nose. Bailey was a great admirer of horses and nudes. He had pictures of both all over the walls of his office. He told Tom that Tig had not been around for over an hour.

Tom paid his rent bill. "Do you want to sell that chestnut?" he asked.

Bailey chewed a match. "I was thinking of seventy-five dollars."

"You were thinking of my tortilla fortune, too, weren't you? . . . Forty, and not a dime more."

Outside, there was a hard clop of hoofs, a grind of tires. Bailey told him complainingly, "He's a half-thoroughbred, Tom, but steady as they come. Give me fifty and we'll call it even."

Before he could answer, a girl called, "Mr. Bailey! Will you open the door?"

Bailey looked at Tom. Between them flashed the knowl-edge of who was outside. ". . . There's a back door,"

Bailey said. "In case you want to leave well enough alone."

Tom grinned. "I'll risk it."

He opened the door. As the buggy turned in, Tom saw Ruth Bannerman on the seat, snug in a dark cape, with a fascinator over her hair.

"Tom!" she said. And with a smile, "If you were waiting for me, we couldn't have timed it better, could we?"

Tom said, "I was just riding up to the mesa to see how many cows Morg left me. My men have been hunting them for a week."

"Your men?" she laughed. "Don't be putting on airs with me, Tom Carmody. I remember when you were saving wages to buy a saddle without splinters."

Tom chuckled. He was at the door when she said, "Why don't you let me drive you up?"

They were looking at each other across the dim aisle. There was something challenging in her half-smile, something that said, *I'm Holt Bannerman's girl, and I'll bet you haven't the nerve to take me away from him again, even for an hour.* . . .

Tom removed his hat and settled it. He told Bailey, "I'll pay you for that horse when I come back."

The mesa road struck through a dense growth of alder, crossed the bridge over the Soledad River and hit a switch-backing climb to the top. They came out on the mesa and Tom put the horse on the faint trail that led to the roundup camp. The smoke of a supper fire fumed in a draw a mile up the line. As they drove, the tough, half-sized piñons and junipers hissed in the wind. Ruth was a small and lovely presence beside him, holding the collar of her cape closed.

"This is like old times, Tom."

"Let's not make it too much like old times. That last buggy ride I've cut out of my memory book."

"Miss me, Tom?" she asked.

"For a while."

"For a while!" Ruth exclaimed.

"Until I got used to the idea that it was all over."

She was smiling a little. "I'd be flattered if you said you went to Mexico to forget me."

"I suppose I did, partly. But partly to make some money. The next time I proposed, it wasn't going to be in chaps held together with baling wire."

"They say you made some money, too."

"I made wages." He did not know why, with Ruth, he felt he had to be on his guard. She had always been frank with him. But today he was aware that she was a Bannerman, that she sank or swam with her father in the matter of Snaketrack.

He asked her about California. She told him about San Francisco and her aunt. They approached a sandy wash. "Hang on," Tom told her. As the buggy lurched into the wash, he locked her in place with a hand gripping the side-bar and his arm braced across her. He turned the horse up the dry streambed and let it trot. Ruth laughed.

"Aren't we formal! You used to do that with an arm around me."

"But you didn't used to be engaged to Morgan Wiley."

"Am I now?"

"Wiley told me it was all set."

She smiled to herself. "He does seem to have that impression. Maybe he got it from Dad. He's working himself to death getting Harper's old place fixed up for us to live in."

"Sounds like he must be getting some encouragement," Tom said pointedly.

"A man like Morg doesn't need encouragement. He takes things for granted. He took it for granted that we were engaged once before, and then I eloped with you. I don't think he loves you for that, Tom."

"If he does, he's never mentioned it. Why did he decide on Harper's place?"

"He didn't. Dad's given me the hay ranch and ten sections adjoining it. It was a peace offering." She settled a little deeper under the bearskin robe as the buggy rattled on. "When I came back he started right out threatening to turn me over his knee. But I turned him over mine. I said there was no use in our trying to live in the same house. We're too much alike. And then I've always had the notion that I'd make a pretty fair rancher myself. So I asked him for some land. That was when he told me about the homestead place—that Clance Harper had fixed up.''

Her eyes were bright. ''It was almost as though the whole thing had been working out this last year. The land has never looked so good, and Clance fixed the house up wonderfully. Dad put in ten sections of other land and said it was mine when I promised to stay on Cross Anchor.''

''So you took it,'' Tom said.

And a great and dismal understanding was being born in him. He was watching her and wondering whether she knew what she was saying about herself.

''Of course I took it! To hear Dad talk, you'd think it was the finest piece of ground in the Territory. It's mainly sentiment with him, but it's grand for raising hay, and the house is comfortable. And it's out of the heavy snows, and right on the edge of Snaketrack.'' She looked up at him with a quirk of mischief in her eyes. ''Could anything be more convenient?''

Tom saw into her, but he kept his smile. ''Who's going to be ranching Snaketrack—me or you?''

Her arm slipped through his. ''Why not both of us? You could call the hay ranch a dowry from a reluctant father-in-law, couldn't you?''

Tom looked up at the notched sunset line of the mountains, smelling the good fragrances of coffee and piñon-smoke from the camp they were nearing. ''You mean that after what happened last time, you'd try it again?''

''Do you think I'm afraid of him?''

''You seemed to be the night he told you to get out of my wagon and into his.''

''. . . Perhaps I was. That was a year ago. But I've learned how to handle him. Tom, if we try it again, we won't be scared off, this time.''

Her voice, her face, were bright with eagerness; and Tom thought ironically that whatever the change Mexico had made in him—the change that Laura did not like— Ruth seemed to find it attractive.

"Ruth," he sighed, "don't you know by now that you never did intend to marry me?"

She gasped. "What do you mean, Tom?"

"I was just a lever you pulled to get your way with your father. You figured you could talk your way into some concessions like the hay ranch—with marriage to me as a threat. But it didn't work. So you ran away, to try it that way."

Ruth sat up stiffly. "I don't like that kind of talk, Tom. I don't find it funny at all."

"Neither do I. The point is, Ruth, that people don't change as fast in a year as you pretend to. They don't go away afraid of anyone as arrogant and stiff-necked as your father, and come back laying down the law to him."

"Tom, I don't follow you," Ruth exclaimed.

"I mean that if you were as tough then as you are now, you wouldn't have let him break us up—unless you'd planned it all the time. And you were tough. Eloping with me was just a feint. It was to show him you meant business."

He looked quickly at her. Her face was quizzical, as if a thought had been uncovered to her which she had not fully examined before. But she narrowed her eyes in angry challenge and held his arm tighter.

"All right, Tom! I'll show you if I meant it. I'll marry you tonight, if you want it!"

Tom laughed. "And you would, too—and sue for divorce on Monday. You'd find me more attractive as a lever than a husband. We'd fight like cats and dogs over my eating the stringiest cows and selling the best. I'm still that sowbelly rancher your dad picked me for."

"If you are, I haven't seen any sign of it," Ruth protested. "You behave more like Billy the Kid than Tom Carmody."

"That's so people will think I am Billy the Kid."

"And being a swashbuckling man, naturally you need a girl in every town."

"Right now," he chuckled, "I don't need a girl in any town."

"But you used to. You used to think you needed me."

"I did, too," he admitted. "I gave up a good job for you and I almost went broke. You couldn't have told me then that I'd ever get over it."

Her eyes were large and her face had softened. "Tom, I don't think you have gotten over it—neither of us has. When all the excitement is over, we're going to realize it. Let's not do anything now to spoil it."

On the dark walls of the gully, a faint firelight glowed. They were approaching the camp, and Tom slowed the horse and said, "That's good advice, Ruth. Let's not try to rush ourselves into trouble, or your father into cutting notches on his gun. It might be all right for you, but I don't want to make a career of being a lever for a girl who wants the moon wrapped in red paper. That's plain talk, but I reckon it's time for it."

She was angry, but now they were drawing up to the fire, and she settled into a tight-lipped silence. The fire burned among saddles, rawhide kyaks, and blanket rolls. Creed Davis squatted near the flames with his Stetson tilted over his face. Across the fire was Clance Harper, his carbine resting on his fat thighs.

"Where's Trinidad?" Tom asked.

Creed's eyes were on the pretty girl beside Tom. "Rode down to town for some creosote a while ago. Some of these critters are going to get the screwworms in the cuts they got that night."

"We're still taking off in the morning?" Clance asked.

"Yes, but only to my place. If I don't make it before then, hold them there. I'll wait another day or two before we go on to Snaketrack."

Harper glanced at the girl and said softly, "I can't guess why . . ."

Tom winked at him and tossed the bottle of whiskey on to the sand at his feet. "Put a little of this in Creed's coffee," he said. "Don't let him get hold of it, or he'll keep you up howling at the moon. *Noches!*"

Running back, the lamps feebly lighting the half-frozen ruts through which the tires cut crisply, they sat far apart.

Entering town, Ruth exclaimed, "Tom, I think you're a fool."

"That's the general opinion on Cross Anchor," Tom said.

Something was in Ruth's face, but before she could voice it, a girl called from the boardwalk just short of the livery stable and Tom reined the horse in. It was Laura Cincinnatus, wearing a dark gown and with a shawl drawn over her head.

"Tom!" she called again. "Can I see you right away?"

Tom was immediately aware of the alarm in her voice.

"Wait for me!" he called.

He gave the horse the ends of the reins and they whirled toward the stable. Tom called to Bailey to open the door, and Ruth spoke curtly. "I see—I didn't realize how it was, Tom. I should think you'd like a little more spice with your sugar, though."

"The mixture seems about right, to me," Tom said.

Ruth quickly laid her hand on his. "Forgive me, Tom. If you didn't remember it from last time, jealousy is one of my failings. . . . Her father is your lawyer, isn't he?"

Tom nodded, and something prompted him to add, "Of course, they're both good friends of mine, too."

—14—

LAURA WAS WAITING where he had seen her, the shawl snugly outlining her face. Tom saw that she was piqued, as well as anxious. "I should think you'd have enough trouble without inviting more," she said.

"Riding with Ruth is no trouble," Tom smiled.

"But it's going to mean trouble before you're through. Any woman could tell you that she's as much a Bannerman as her father—and maybe a little more."

Tom laughed, now. "You can't have all the pebbles on the beach, Papoose. You're supposed to throw back the ones you don't want to the other girls. You can't have me around forever, like one of your Dad's Indian trophies."

Laura tilted her chin. "It's not that at all! It's none of my business what girls you squire around. But I wish you wouldn't go riding with a girl who's just getting you out of town for her father."

Tom's face froze. "What's up?"

"Bannerman's with Tig Jones, at his cabin! I saw them going up the street together just before you left town. I went after you, but Mr. Bailey told me you and Ruth had gone for a drive."

Alarm stroked like a bell in Tom. He had one bitter thought of Ruth, tolling him out of the way while her father worked on Tig, and then his whole need was for action. He turned and started back to the stable. Laura was calling after him:

"This once, Tom, take some advice—go in like a lamb, even if you come out like a lion."

He saddled the chestnut he had bought from Bailey and loped to the cross street on which Tig lived, cut past a woodyard and a few homes behind slatternly fences. The early night tinkled with frost. He came to the little rock house in which the old man made his bachelor's existence. Lamplight brushed the windows. Bannerman's big dun stood in the yard. Breathless, Tom dismounted.

Then for the first time he thought of what Laura had said. It sank down through him like a cool drink of water. It was steadying. He took time to light a cigar, and all the angry things he had been going to say to both of them lost their edge. He saw a cleverer way to play out his anger.

Through the window he could see the small room with its unmade cot, its litter of table and chairs and cookstove, and the big bluish jug on one chair which housed Jones' rattlesnake. Holt Bannerman sat at the table. After a moment Tom smiled.

He rapped on the door and pushed it open. "Tig!" he said. "Been looking for you, old timer."

Lean and scowling, the old man came forward. His goatee was untrimmed, his eyes were irascible, and—Tom thought—a little ashamed. But Tig's half-shout was full of accusation.

"*You've* been lookin' for *me!* I been ahuntin' you for three days. Why in hell didn't you stay around, if you wanted to lease my ranch?"

Not answering, holding his temper, Tom looked past him, at Bannerman. "Got company, eh?"

"But I got a new lessee, too. I gave you your chance, Tom, but all I got was stalls. I'm headin' for California tomorrow."

"Is the lease signed?" Tom asked.

"As good as."

"I'll come in and congratulate the winner," Tom said. "This ought to buy me a drink, eh?"

Bannerman sat with his elbows on the table. He had a drink cupped in his hand. There was less of triumph than of irritation in his face. Tom looked at him, at the walnut planes of his face, implacable and shrewd, at the wise and ruthless eyes, and he thought, *I picked a man my own size, by God!*

94

Bannerman took a swallow of liquor. "I hear you changed your mind about moving onto Snaketrack. Saved us both a lot of trouble, eh?"

"I haven't changed my mind about Chunk McAllister," Tom said. "I'm going to get him. And he'll talk before they lock him up."

"I hope so," Bannerman said flatly.

The casual host, Tig Jones insisted, "Put Bucktooth off that chair and set. Cup on the sink. You talk this real good, Tommy. You see my spot, don't you?"

"I see mine, too," sighed Tom, pouring an inch of liquor into a china cup. He added a half-glass of cold spring water. He placed the big glass jug holding the snake on the floor. The snake made his small and deathly whisper. Tom put his boottoe against the glass as he sat down. The snake struck with a soft thud.

"I can't talk you into waiting another day?" Tom said. "The money might be up tomorrow."

Bannerman struck the table. "Why should he wait? He can have his money tonight. Tig's doing what any sensible man would do."

But Tig's eyes were ashamed as he rolled a cigarette with lanky fingers. He could not have forgotten that a few nights ago, he had thrown whiskey in the Cross Anchor man's face; that he had held a pistol on him and threatened to fire it. And now he was crawfishing on all he had said.

"You see, Tom, everything's so damned mixed up. Man don't know where he stands. Here it is the last of October, and winter a-blowin' on its hands. I'm gettin' out. And this is cash—tonight if I want it."

"You can't use it tonight," Tom pointed out, "and maybe I can give you cash tomorrow. You know," he said, "one thing they've always said about you is that your word's worth a hundred cents on the dollar. I brought ten thousand dollars' worth of cattle up here on your word. Are you going to make them out a liar, now?"

Remorse touched Tig's old face. He moistened the corners of his mouth and wiped them with a forefinger. "There's Trinidad, too . . ." he complained.

"What about Pete?"

"They're saying he's put the hooks into you for some of that money of yours. That it's rustlin' money."

"Who's saying that?" Tom asked quietly.

"Bannerman," Tig said.

"Do you want to say that to me?" Tom asked the rancher.

Color charged Bannerman's face, but he kept his glance steadily on Tom. "I only repeated what they're all saying."

"I'll give you something else to repeat: I can whip any man that says I don't own every dollar of my money."

Bannerman's grin went past Tom to Tig. "I've even heard it said it was in rebel pesos—worth about the same as wallpaper."

Looking at Tig, Tom saw his bitterness, his confusion. He reached out and put his toe against the jug. "Want to take a chance on six bits of hard cash, Tig?"

"Make it a buck," grinned Tig.

Tom held his hand against the glass. The rattlesnake smashed softly against it. Tom's hand leaped out of range, and he chuckled ruefully and stood up to grab a dollar out of his pocket. He spun it to Tig. Then he lifted the jug by the neck. "You know, a man could get attached to a moneymaker like this."

"Bucktooth," chuckled Jones, "is my sweetheart and my banker."

Tom carried the bottle to the sink and poured another drink. He carried the jug around the table and hooked a chair to him with his toe. Bannerman watched him. His fingers slowly, warily, lathed a cigar between them.

"Damn it," Tom said impatiently, "it looks like I ought to be entitled to twenty-four hours' notice, don't it?"

Bannerman's laugh was short and deep. "Let's not talk about twenty-four-hour notice—after what almost happened to me! Rest the land all summer—to give you fatter cows."

From a window, Tig watched the sprinkle of early lights in the village. He did not speak. After a moment Tom finished his drink, walked behind Bannerman, and with a quick motion set the snake on the table before Bannerman. The sandrattler hissed, its dusty body lashed forward at the glass.

"God damn it!"

Bannerman's hand slashed at the snake. His hand struck the glass and the jug was falling. Tom exclaimed and lunged forward to catch it, but it was gone, crashing on the hard earth floor before he could reach it. On the floor were a thousand glinting slivers of glass, a scatter of sand, and something drab but virulent lashing in the midst of it. Bannerman's boot was only a foot away. He was hurling himself aside with an oath, tugging at his Colt. Tig's shout was savage as a gunshot.

Bannerman's Colt bellowed. The lamp went out.

Tignal Jones was shouting in insane fury: "If you've killed that snake!—"

A light came up. Tom had struck a match. In the dim light they could see the snake writhing. Bannerman's bullet had torn the snake's head from its body. Slowly he pouched the gun, still shaken.

Tom lit the lamp. With a start then he strode across the cabin. A holstered Navy pistol hung near Tig's cot. Tig was savagely yanking at it. Tom caught him and wrestled him to the bed. The old man was shouting his drunken fury.

"The best friend a man ever had! Shot down like a dog!"

Tom turned his head. "Out!" he said to Bannerman. "For God's sake *out!*"

Bannerman took a heavy shortcoat from the back of his chair, but came forward to plead with the old man. "Good Lord, Tig, what would you have done? He set that snake against my arm, deliberately—"

"I'll damn well show you what I'd'a'done!" shouted Tig.

Bannerman stared for an instant at Carmody. Then he went out and shut the door with a crash.

—15—

IN THE GREAT WESTERN SALOON, the frost-bitten veterans of Marshal Ridge's posse were drinking to Chunk McAllister's death by starvation in the mountains where they had lost him. A half-dozen of them, gaunt and unshaven, just in, stood at the bar. Morgan Wiley stood beside Marshal Ridge, though he had not been a posseman—he was, thought Tom, merely Bannerman's agent at this wake. Pete Trinidad stood alone at the end, near the trestled beer-barrel, listening. Seeing Tom enter, he lifted a hand slightly to signify, *Listen to this. . . .*

Tom joined him but waved off the bartender. He heard the baritone exasperation of Gus Hurley, the gunsmith.

"A catamount couldn't track that lunatic! He could take a herd of mustangs down Front Street without leaving a trail a hound could follow."

Stern and tired, Ridge poured whiskey into his glass. Red Murphy stopped before him with his hands on his hips, his dish towel apron soiled from the long day. Murphy had never been a Bannerman partisan, and Tom saw irritation in his face.

"When did you start losin' trails, Mike?" the saloon-keeper asked. "I remember when there was only one man in the county you'd take your hat off to for trackin'."

Ridge slowly looked up. "Who was that, Red?"

"Jim Shaniko."

Tom was conscious of Trinidad laying his hand on the bar, the long fingers flattening out.

"I still take off my hat to Jim," Ridge said. "If he'd

been along, we wouldn't have lost Chunk. That's why I'm sending him out tonight."

Morg Wiley said in the flat silence: "Jim'll bring him in."

Then there was the kind of whiskey-fed talk which bred legends: Someone remembered how Shaniko had tracked French Jack, the piano player Brophy had hired one winter who killed his sweetheart. Shaniko had followed him for a week and brought him in more dead than alive. Other men remembered small things Shaniko had said or done, so that the big Cross Anchor range boss began to sound like Wild Bill Hickok himself. Tom smiled, and by him a man who knew all about Jim Shaniko gently rubbed at the varnished bartop with his fingertips.

Trinidad suddenly finished his drink and stepped back from the bar. Tom's hand caught his wrist. "Pete," he said.

"'Sta bien," the Mexican soothed him. But as he started down the bar, Tom was beside him.

Trinidad touched the marshal's arm. Ridge turned, unsurprised. They looked into each other's eyes, and at last the marshal said, "Hello, Pete. I wondered when you'd come say hello."

The other possemen, the regular patrons, even Murphy, looked at Trinidad with the respect saved for a gunman of notoriety. Trinidad basked in it—Tom saw how he let his right shoulder slouch a little more toward the basket-woven holster on his thigh. In the backbar, he studied the reflection of a dark-skinned, good-looking man who wore his sideburns long and trimmed his mustache to a hair-line. Trinidad smiled, sleek, expensively dressed in gray-and-black-striped trousers and a coat piped with grosgrain.

"How you been, Marshal?" Trinidad smiled.

"Good, Pete. How you been?"

"Good. How's my friend, Jim Shaniko?"

"Fat and sassy," Ridge smiled. "Fat and sassy."

"Is not good a deputy should get fat, Marshal," said Trinidad. "A fat deputy is a slow deputy, and a slow deputy don't live long."

"Shall we tell him you said that?" Morg Wiley cut in.

"Why scare him?" asked Trinidad, smiling.

"I don't think it'd scare him," Wiley said. His face was full of contempt, of an urge toward violence, though he grinned with his wide mouth and dark-browed eyes.

"All right, cut it out!" Ridge rapped. "Isn't there enough going on without you two startin' to circle like alley curs? Pete, I want a talk with you at my office sometime soon. Say tomorrow."

"Am I still on probation?" Trinidad asked.

"No, but there's a couple of things—"

"If you want to talk to me," Trinidad said, suddenly bald of humor, "swear out a warrant. The only talking you and I will ever do will be across a warrant. I don't want nobody warning me not to do this and that. I'm working for Tom Carmody. I'm as straight as I always was. If there's any trouble, it won't be me that starts it."

"It better not be," said the marshal. "Or by God—"

"Or what?" Trinidad smiled, after a moment.

"Hasta luego," Ridge said tightly, "See you soon, Pete."

"Hasta luego," said Trinidad.

. . . They walked fifty feet into the freezing darkness. Tom chuckled. "Billy the Kid's right-hand-arm, eh, Pete?"

Trinidad was still swollen with the success of the moment. He stopped to light a black *papel orozuz* cigarette. "They didn't give me no Spik talk tonight, Tomas. You see them looking at me?"

"Sure. Trying to see how you'll look in hemp."

Across the street, a packhorse stood before Bailey's Livery Stable. Splinters of light gleamed in the door of the barn. "Where'd you leave your horse?" Tom asked the Mexican.

"At the hotel rack. I left a jug of creosote there."

"Want to take a ride?"

"I figured to. Back to the herd."

"You'll like this ride better. . . . I was just with Tig and Bannerman. I think I won another couple of days' grace. I'm banking on it, anyhow, because I'm liable to be out of town tomorrow."

Trinidad's face was sharp with interest. "Where you going?"

"After Shaniko. Maybe I'm wrong, Pete. I don't think it's a tracking expedition at all. I think it's a rendezvous. I think Bannerman paid Chunk to make trouble, and now that it's got out of hand he's got to get him out of the territory. But I'd like to bring that 'coon back alive and talking."

Drawing on the cigarette, Trinidad said, "How we going to follow him at night?"

"He'll stay on the road for a while. After that we'll have to do the best we can." Hearing voices in the stable, he said, "Go back to the hotel and wait."

Tom crossed to the livery barn. He stood outside a moment, trying to hear what Jim Shaniko was saying. The horse at the rack was loaded with two deep rawhide *aparejos*. Tom rapped one with his knuckles. Frowning, then, he put a palm under it and lifted. It was empty. Yet the cases were lashed down, ready to travel.

He stood there until Shaniko's voice said, "Well, I ain't getting any closer to him standin' here, Harry. Take it easy."

"You too, Jim," Bailey said.

Shaniko slid the door aside and started out, leading his pony. His face was red with cold. His brows were yellow as rope and his eyes were a dilute blue, and Tom thought that his mouth looked like a healed scar. It was a face that wanted a fist.

Shaniko made a sudden, involuntary movement, and Tom said, "No!"

Shaniko's hand slid from the bulge of the gun under his coat. "All right. Here I am," he said tauntingly.

"Come on out," Tom said.

Shaniko's eyes toughened. He knew the trick—catching a man in a doorway to get in first lick, which was apt to be the last. But he could not back up at this point without seeming to be afraid. "Sure," he said.

He moved into the slot, the pony behind him. For a moment he was squeezed there, Tom just a couple of feet away, waiting. Then Tom murmured, "Relax, Jim! You look nervous. Why should I take you on before I'm ready?"

Shaniko shrugged and smirked. "Sure, Tom. Only don't take all winter getting ready."

Tom watched him take up the lead-rope of the packhorse, mount his pony, and ride down the road. "You're pizen mean these days," Bailey chuckled.

Tom pulled out a clasp-purse and paid for the pony he had bought that afternoon. "You get that way, lone-wolfing," he said.

He picked up Trinidad and they rode to the side street, turning west to the wagon road. At the junction where the road turned south, Carmody halted, listening. There was no sound of hoofs. Shaniko was out of earshot. The Mexican stirred restlessly.

"How we going to track this guy in the dark?"

"I don't figure we'll have to. Shaniko'll camp somewhere. I've got a sneaking idea where Chunk is. But Jim won't be walking in on him at night—not the way Chunk is with a rifle. He'll camp out and meet him early."

About three miles out, a spine of rock slanted from the hills. Tom climbed to a vantage point. Far out on the mesa a fire burned. It was a bold fire, built by a man who did not expect to be tracked. Shaniko's coffee would be boiling; his blankets would be absorbing the fire-heat before he rolled into them.

Tom climbed down. "We ride, Pete! Shaniko's out on Mesa Grande. I'm banking that he's making for the big corral at Cibolo Creek. All the cow-work's been done over there. It's as good a place to hole up as any. If we can coyote in close enough, we'll be around to shake his hand when he rides in."

—16—

IT WAS TWO YEARS since Tom Carmody had ridden Mesa Grande, this great sprawl of Bannerman's range which ran twenty miles out into the *llanos*. In his mind the mesa lay like a map: the kinks of Turkey Creek and the hardscrabble ridges of the Blacks Hills; the brushy tangles of Cibolo Creek. Except when the snows were deep, it was easy range.

They circled Jim Shaniko's fire widely, wanting him to have no indication that he was not out here alone. It might be a bonafide tracking expedition he was on, but Tom could not forget the empty kyacks on his packhorse. A man did not carry empty packs without reason.

They reached the headwaters of Cibolo Creek, a sandy gully into which drained a dozen rivulets. They put their ponies into it and cautiously followed a cattle trail for a half-mile until they came to a dead cottonwood on the north bank.

Tom told Trinidad, "It's only a quarter-mile from here. We'll leave the horses."

As they paced ahead, ice tinkled in the stream. Gaunt fingers of brush reached for their boots. Cautious as he was, Tom suddenly felt his spur-chain caught by a branch. He twisted for balance, but stumbled and sprawled in the rocks. Trinidad hunched. *"Maldito!"*

In the cramped instant of waiting, someone could be heard moving, not far ahead. Then without warning, a rifle crashed and an avalanche of echoes cascaded down the gully. They had heard the slug strike in the brush and stones; and they lay there.

Tom's heart seemed to swell and pulse until it filled his chest. He lay exactly where he had fallen. In the back of his mind was the realization of what had happened. Chunk McAllister had made camp a hundred feet from the shack, anticipating trackers.

After a while, no more shots having come, his hand closed about a damp stone. It was lightly cemented with ice. He pulled it loose and threw it into the creek. The stone clattered among the rocks and ice and was still. Trinidad groaned.

"Por Dios, Tom, what you do?"

"Varmints don't lie low when a gun goes off," Tom whispered. "They get to hell out."

The moment tightened like wire. But McAllister did not fire again. After a while they heard small movements, as of someone settling down.

They dug in miserably in frost and damp.

WITH THE PATIENCE of his people, Trinidad squatted by a tree and chewed smoking tobacco while night drained out of the sky. He had a Christmas-Eve look, thought Tom. In the morning he would find an old enemy in his stocking. He had wanted it to be on the main street of Soledad, but he did not seem disappointed. He was going to get back at Shaniko for his two years in Santa Fe prison. He was going to fire a shot for all "Spiks."

Daylight started as a watery light in the east. They saw the gray prison of branches they were in. Ahead, they could make out a rock shack beside a stone corral. Branding irons hung from the low branches of a tree. Remains of old beef carcasses, slaughtered by roundup crews, lay gauntly in the brush.

Tom heard movement. Chunk appeared from a thicket, a bearded, hunch-shouldered figure in ragged horsehide jacket and jeans stiff with grease. With two fingers, he blew his nose on the ground, wiped his hand and walked to the creek. He straightened for a moment and stared around. Then with his bootheel he punched a hole in the thin ice of the creek and dipped a handful of water. He drank it and shook his hand dry, swearing against the cold.

Now he went into the cabin. After a few minutes a pencil of smoke rose from the stone chimney. Tom tried sighting on the door down the browned barrel of the Henry rifle. But twigs and branches robbed him of a clean shot.

It was about eight when they heard a horse on the trail above the cabin.

Moving like an animal, McAllister slid out the back door of the cabin and slipped into the brush. A pony scuffed down the rocky trail behind the line-shack and a man whistled, "When Johnny Comes Marching Home." Leading the packhorse, Deputy Marshal Jim Shaniko rode into the yard. He sat the horse quietly. After a moment he called, "Does a man named Jones live here?"

Brush crackled. McAllister reappeared, rifle in hand, a fat grin on his whiskered face. "I'm Jones," he said.

"I've got some groceries for you, Jones," said Shaniko. "Got coffee on?"

"Strong and hot, by damn, strong and hot!" said Chunk. He ran up, delighted as a child.

As the hunter went inside, Shaniko looked after him for a moment. He did something odd. He cocked his Colt without removing it from the holster. Trinidad made a sound in his throat. Tom came straight up on his knees.

While the deputy threw off the lashings of the rawhide packs, McAllister brought a tin cup of coffee to the porch. He placed it on the dirt floor by a box. "You're late, Jim," he complained.

"Late hell. This is the day. I left town last night."

Chunk pulled a wattle of skin under his chin. "Thought it was yesterday. I kinda forgot. . . . Everything all right in town?"

Shaniko winked. "We're handling everything, Chunk. You just lose yourself in the mountains and turn up in Texas. Everything's fine."

In wistful reflection, the hunter stood by a stanchion while Shaniko wearily let himself down on the box and stirred the coffee.

"That old man," Chunk said, "shore usta give me hell, Jim! I was sweet on that Agency squaw, but he'd run me out every time I'd try to see her. Like I wasn't fit for a Hickareea squaw."

"Well, anyone would know he would come after you after what you done up there, an' now he's deader'n a mackerel."

"Dead!" said Chunk.

"What the hell'd you think?" Shaniko retorted. "You hit a man with a .45–790 slug, something's got to give."

"Yeah, but I—I never shot to kill him. And I can shoot the dandruff off a gnat's head without creasing him."

"Well, you shot the dandruff off the judge's!" Shaniko told him.

Suddenly the hunter said, "Damn Morg Wiley!"

Shaniko regarded him without expression. "What's Morg got to do with it?"

"He give me the whiskey. He knowed I'd git in trouble—I hold this ag'in Wiley," he said intently.

"Then you're a damned fool," said the range boss. "Morg could have taken you in the other day when he spotted you out here. But he didn't. He told you to lie low and he'd help you get away if the judge died."

McAllister's face was red and sullen. "Like hell he could have took me in! I had him under my sights while we talked, and he knew it."

"Well, he could have gone back and got Ridge, couldn't he?"

Thinking about it, Chunk slowly let himself down on the porch and rested his hands on his knees. "I reckon so, Jim. But he never give me whiskey before. If it hadn't been for that, I wouldn't have gone after that squaw, and if I hadn't, then the jedge wouldn't have tried to take me in."

Shaniko sighed and sipped the coffee. "Next you'll be blamin' the man that stilled the whiskey. It's over and done, Chunk. Forget it. Figger Cincinnatus had it coming. . . . Look at your vittles," he said cheerfully.

Chunk, after a moment, almost disinterestedly opened one of the rawhide cases. Tom saw his head turn. "It's empty, Jim. How come?"

"Look in the other."

The bounty hunter stood up and opened the other pack. He slowly turned, his hands hanging. "They're both empty."

Shaniko had drawn the cocked gun while McAllister opened the packs. His red, blond-browed face was taut. "*This* ain't empty, Chunk. Them's all the vittles you're going to need. I arrest you for the murder of Judge Myron Cincinnatus.''

In a loud, querulous voice, Chunk said, ''What the hell you doin', Jim?''

''Raise your hands!'' Shaniko said, sitting rigidly on the box.

Chunk dropped to one knee and his hand scratched at his Colt. The gunshot was a single pulse of thunder in the yard. McAllister went back on his haunches. A dense pall of gunsmoke rolled over him. Again he came up on his knees, the Colt in his hand. Shaniko fired a second shot through the smudge of powder-smoke. He fired a third, with the coldblooded air of a man shooting at a tin can.

Tom had sat frozen. But now Trinidad lunged up, his rifle snapping to his shoulder. It was a long shot and a brushy one. The gun roared. Twigs crackled, a single large leaf twirled down. Beside Jim Shaniko, adobe plaster puffed from the wall.

Tom thrust the Mexican aside and began running up the rocky trail beside the creek. Shaniko shouted something. His spurs chimed in the yard. Tom plunged across the creek for a shot at him. A stone, slick with ice, turned his boot and he was down in a tangle of brush like barbed wire. Pete came crashing along, jumped him and reached the sandy bank. There was a stutter of hoofs as Tom scrambled up.

A rifle cracked again. As he ran out, he collided with Trinidad, standing there. Trinidad went into a twisting fall. Tom looked at him in surprise. He watched him writhing slowly on the ground. Then he straightened and stared at the man loping out of the yard. Suddenly he brought the gun up. Bent over the pommel, Shaniko was slashing behind the cabin. Tom fired. Shaniko was out of sight, hammering up the trail.

When Tom rode back from tracking Shaniko up the mesa trail, Trinidad was sitting against a boulder, trying to roll a cigarette.

''*Dios y cielo!* A shot at him! Standin' there like a treed cougar—and I missed!''

108

"You never killed a cougar that way," Tom said. "Lay back, now."

Trinidad's boot was deep with blood. Tom found the wound high up, four inches below the knee. It had cut a slot across the outside of his calf.

The flow of blood stanched, he helped Trinidad mount. It was a little after ten when they left, Trinidad riding ahead, Tom following with McAllister's body across a packhorse.

They stopped three times to let the Mexican rest. Tom would build a fire and remove Trinidad's boot to let the circulation quicken. In this slow fashion, they reached Soledad in midafternoon, gaunt with cold and fatigue.

Carmody rode past Front Street, making for the marshal's office. Suddenly Trinidad broke his long silence. His voice was bitter with self-accusation.

"What's he gonna do, Tom?"

"I don't know. If I was in his spot, and had guts, I'd come back to town and say I'd tracked McAllister down and a couple of men jumped me as I took him. But if I *didn't* have guts—I reckon I'd keep riding."

"Then he'll keep riding."

Tom tried to see through the dusty panes of Ridge's office. "Maybe so. . . . Pete, you cut on to the hotel and take a room. I'll send Doctor Brough over. I'll fix this up with Ridge."

Trinidad shrugged. "What's it matter? What's anything matter, to a fella that can't shoot no straighter than me?"

"Maybe you'll get another chance. But not in this town, Pete."

As the Mexican jogged away, Ridge stepped on to the walk. Seeing the packhorse behind Carmody, he put his hand up to remove his cigar.

"Tom!" he said. "Who under the sun—"

"Chunk McAllister," Tom said.

"My God!" Ridge said. He stepped forward and looked into the dead face. "Where'd you find him?"

"At Bannerman's line-shack on Cibolo Creek."

"You had your guts to tackle him. You're lucky to be here."

"I didn't kill him. Shaniko did."

"Shaniko? Where is he, Tom? You don't mean—"

"I don't know where he is. Trinidad and I followed him out there last night. He was taking off with empty pack-saddles for this hunting expedition, and I got inquisitive. This morning he rode up and shook Chunk's hand and they passed the time of day. We were laying in the brush. He said, 'Here's your vittles. Now get out of sight.' When Chunk found out they were empty, Jim shot him—Chunk didn't have any more chance than Cincinnatus had."

Ridge looked at the gopherish, blood-choked mouth of Chunk McAllister. "You don't murder a would-be murderer, Tom," he frowned. "You take him—dead or alive."

"Even if you've made a rendezvous with him?"

"What do you mean?"

"I heard enough to know that Wiley'd come across Chunk out there the other day. Don't call it an accident— Wiley'd given Chunk the whiskey, and he knew his habits well enough to figure about where he'd hole up—some spot where the cattle-work was finished and he could lay low. Wiley promised Chunk he'd bring vittles for a get-away across the *llanos*, if the judge died."

"But Cincinnatus didn't!" Ridge protested.

"No, but Shaniko told Chunk he had. He wanted to rattle him, to see how much Chunk had figured out about it all. Chunk started talking. He said enough that Shaniko knew he'd have to close his mouth for good."

Ridge began throwing off the ropes that held the hunter across the pack-animal. He stopped to face Tom impatiently.

"That's a lot of figurin', Tom. But what's it add up to? Why'd Wiley prime him for trouble?"

"To get the judge out of town. He knew Cincinnatus would have to go out to bring him in. Remember, you told me yourself it was out of your territory? But maybe he didn't know how far it would go. So Chunk had to go, too."

"Wiley had no stake in getting Cincinnatus out of town. What difference would it make to him?"

Tom smiled. "Don't you figure that one, either?"

Studying him, Ridge after a moment turned back to the

packhorse. "You mean Bannerman had a stake in tolling him away, and Wiley works for Bannerman? Maybe so, Tom. But would you lock a man up on evidence like that? You could be wrong, you know."

Tom's eyes hardened. *Go easy . . . go easy!* The old refrain. He saw Ridge weighing out his life on apothecary's scales.

"Mike, for God's sake!" he exploded. "You can swear out a warrant for Shaniko, can't you? You can take my word and Trinidad's that we heard what we heard and saw Shaniko shoot Chunk in cold blood, can't you? Will you go that far out on the limb?"

"Sure, but I won't draw the conclusions you want me to. Not until I see better proof than you give me."

"All right! Can I count on it that you'll post a warrant for Shaniko's arrest, on suspicion of murder?"

"Right now," Ridge said.

"That's good," Tom told him, "because Shaniko put a bullet into Trinidad, too, and if Shaniko don't leave the country or get himself locked up, Pete's going to kill him. That's for sure."

—18—

DOCTOR BROUGH BROUGHT his brown cowhide bag and a worried frown to Pete Trinidad's room in the hotel. "Treating gunshot wounds is getting to be the biggest part of my practice," he complained.

Trinidad had already put a pint of whiskey between himself and the pain. He took the cauterizing of the wound with mild Spanish curses. Tom, frowning over a cigarette, wished he might have the blessing of drunkenness to ease out his tension. From the window, he could look down on the darkening street. A gang of punchers went by at a ringing lope; three women conversed excitedly on the walk. Walking rapidly, a man crossed from the hotel to the far side of the street and turned south toward the jail.

Soledad knew of Chunk McAllister's return.

Brough finished with the Mexican. "Stay off your leg," he ordered. "After she starts suppuratin', everything ought to go along nice. I'll leave you some pills. Take one now and another if you wake up."

"Sure," Pete said, and when the doctor had left he leaned over and dropped them into the chamber pot.

"About one A.M.," Tom said drily, "you'll be wishing you'd kept those."

Trinidad was in a state of dreamy good nature. "Bounty hunters don't sleep, Tomas."

"If Shaniko's got a brain the size of a twenty-two cartridge," Tom said, "he'll be halfway to Las Vegas by now."

"But he ain't. That's what I'm counting on. . . . I wonder if your money's come up yet!" he speculated.

"*You* wonder!" Tom took his coat from a chair. "While you wonder, I aim to find out."

"What you gonna do if it has?"

"What do you think I'm going to do?"

"What about the little general?" asked Trinidad. "What if he shows up for his money?"

Tom scowled. He had almost put this worry to rest, but now Trinidad dragged it out in its death-clothes. "The general and I," he said, "will have to work something out."

The porch of the Great Western was set back from the street and railed off. Tom stood among the empty rockers stirring slightly in the wind. The street's briskness was not all the fault of the freezing wind. Chunk's death was part of it; and the warrant for Jim Shaniko. The street was a pulse, and it was pounding. Tom faced into a corner to light a cigarette, and as he turned back he saw a woman ascending the hotel steps. As she reached for the door, he said quickly:

"Maybe he isn't there, lady."

Startled, Laura Cincinnatus turned. "Oh—Tom!" She came toward him, then, and Tom knew at once that something was wrong.

"Is it your father?" he asked quickly.

She shook her head, letting the shawl down on to her shoulders, exposing the faint highlights of her hair. She moved one of the rockers and sat down. "Sit down, Tom," she told him. As he did so, she asked, "Have you talked to Phil Cornelius?"

There was a quick bounce of excitement in him, yet in an instant it was gone, and he knew what she was going to say and was scarcely moved by it. "The money's here," he said.

"It came in an hour ago! Cornelius came up to tell us, and after we heard from Doctor Brough that you and Trinidad were back, I decided you ought to know. Tom, we *are* glad for you."

And she was glad, he knew—glad enough to hope that she and her father had been wrong. "I wish—" he sighed; and hesitated, not sure that he wanted to say it. He heard the tin gaiety of Brophy's mechanical piano; he scented frying supper meat on the wind.

"What do you wish?" she prompted.

He wished he had gone more slowly, as she had wanted him to. But he could not bring himself to say it, not when Trinidad's general might never show up; not when he could still be proved right.

"Maybe I wish it was twice as much," he said grinning.

Laura took his hand. "Tom, what is it? What's wrong? Is it about—seeing Chunk killed? This isn't the way I thought you'd act. Dad said you'd stand on a chair and shout a couple of mountains down."

Tom spun his cigarette into the street. "It's happened so gradually that I can't get excited over it. You'd think a peso fortune would excite a sowbelly rancher like me. But it's been too long happening."

"Is there anything wrong with the money?" Laura asked quietly.

Tom shook his head. "Nobody else has claimed it."

"Then I think you ought to get Tig quickly and bring him to the office. Dad said to tell you he'd finished his opinion on Carmody's Gold, and it's all right."

Tom smiled. "What's his opinion on Shaniko? Will he give himself up?"

"He thinks that Shaniko will come skulking in some time and surrender. But he said to watch out for Morgan Wiley when Ruth announces her engagement to you."

"You'd better watch me, too, because it will be news to me."

She tilted her head, dubiously. "You looked awfully cozy, coming in from the ride with her last night."

"That's because she was doing a job for her old man. You were right about her. She was the bait to get me out of town while he signed up Tig."

"I don't think that's right, Tom. I know I said it before, but I'm convinced Ruth is really in love with you. You've changed—and she likes the change. I think she'd marry you even if you lost Snaketrack.''

"Ruth," Tom said, "will never love anybody that much. Enough to marry him rich, maybe, but not poor. How many women would, as far as that goes?''

She scolded him with a look, and Tom partially retracted it. "Just the opinion of a man who loved unwisely and too well. On the other hand, we have the kind of woman who'll marry town marshals, and have to patch his election shirts every year—the ones with the pockets worn out from carrying cigars. . . . Do you really love him, Laura?'' he asked her; and then he wished he had not asked it, because he did not want to know.

"Don't *you* think I love him?" she countered.

"I don't think you'd get engaged to any man you didn't love," Tom said.

"We're not engaged," Laura said, after a moment. Tom looked blankly at her; and she added, "I've not been asked yet."

A quick hope tried to rise in Tom. "Papoose," he sighed, "you'd be asked right now, if this were last year. If I were going to a home-sweet-home, instead of a fortress, I'd be carrying you off and to the devil with Ridge.''

She sniffed. "Just because my father's a good lawyer.''

"No. I thought I'd been wearing it like a derby, Laura. I thought everybody'd seen it. It's a little hard to phrase, but I guess I mean I love you.''

"Tom," she said, in gentle reproof, softly smiling at him. "Tom, dear, you love just the way you do everything else. In a rush. In love this week, out of love next.''

He wanted to smile, to make it half a joke, but he could not. He could only hold her hands and tell her. "No. Not this time. You're something special, Laura.''

"But last year you gave up a job and everything else for a girl—and now you say you aren't interested in her! Are you sure you know yourself, Tom?''

"I'm getting to," Tom sighed. "I'm getting to know your marshal, too. He surprised me today. He issued a warrant for Jim Shaniko. That'll make Bannerman hot enough to break him. I wish I could have kept on hating him, but all I can hold against him is that he gave Pete Trinidad a bad shake, and even that wasn't on purpose."

He watched her, hesitated. She rose and pulled the shawl over her head. "I'm glad you feel that way, Tom. Because he's as honest, and—and good as a woman could want. Will you bring Tig up as soon as you find him?"

The intimate instant was ended. "Have a pot of black coffee ready to sober him up," Tom said. "And save a cup for me." He watched her go down the steps and hurry up the boardwalk, and stood for a long while before he left the porch.

In the Great Western, Tignal Jones stood among a half-dozen listless patrons at the bar. Coming into the dry heat of the room, Tom glanced over it with a sense of reconnoitering—seeing at once that Morgan Wiley sat with two Cross Anchor men at a table near the tonsorial booth at the front, where Red Murphy cut hair in slack hours. Wiley had a stub of cigar in the corner of his mouth; his thick-haired hands dealt poker stolidly. He did not see Tom enter, but lowered the cigar to sop the chewed end in a shot-glass of brandy and again raise it to his mouth.

There should be a ceremony for this, Tom thought—the changing of an order, the passing of a cattle empire. But he could think of nothing less suited to his mood than fanfare. He wanted to lay the money before Jones and tell Bannerman he could go to hell. He wanted to do this and go out and take over at Snaketrack, to raise cattle and forget about Ruth and Laura and the year that was past.

Walking into the room, he followed the line of the bar and stood with a puncher who was watching Jones and the saloon-keeper. Tom saw, with a twist of sympathy, what Jones was doing. He had three walnut shells on the bar. His veined hands finished moving them and he said to Murphy:

"There, by Joe! Whichun this time?"

Murphy, seeing Tom, winked and rifled a thin sheaf of bills. "Middle one ag'in," he said.

Tig scowled and turned over the shell. A small rubber

pea was exposed. Murphy chuckled and picked up a dollar lying on the bar. "Tough," he said.

Tig clenched his fist and savagely clumped it down on the shells, one after the other. He swept the shards from the bar, while the cowboys laughed. "There won't never be another skin-game like Bucktooth!" a man said.

Suddenly Tig turned back to Murphy. His rutted, goateed face was sly. He wore a black stock, stained with tobacco ash and food, and now he took the cigar from the saloon-keeper's hand and said, "Will you cover a ten-spot that I can't hold this hot cigar ag'in my stock without burning it?"

Murphy said, "No, because you've got a silver dollar under the cloth to take the heat away. Tig, you'd better give it up till spring, when the snakes come out of hibernation. You're more of a snake charmer than you are a magician."

At that moment Jones saw Tom. He saw in him a target for his frustration. He pointed a crooked finger at him, his face twisting in accusation. "Tom, we're quits! You've had a week. Bannerman may be a pig, but he's cash. I'm going to him tomorrow. I'm getting the hell out of this town."

At the table, Morg Wiley was on his feet. Tom saw him lounging forward. "Hang around, Tig," Wiley said. "I'll get him for you."

Tom turned his back to the bar, his elbows caught on it, smiling at the ramrod, then glancing at Tignal Jones. "Take it easy, Tig," he said. "My money's in."

Wiley stopped short, his hands falling to his sides. Tig uttered a whoop. "Belly up, boys! The king is dead—long live Tom Carmody!"

Tom had two drinks with him before Tig shouted, "Where the hell's everybody? Somebody stick your head out the door and let 'em know Tig Jones is settin' 'em up!"

"Can we do that later?" Tom asked him. "The judge is waiting up to close this for us."

Jones frowned. "Well, it needn't take ten minutes. . . . Say, I hear you done for that idiot, McAllister!"

"Pete and I brought him in," Tom said. "Give Shaniko

credit for the kill. He gave Chunk the Shaniko Special—right where the suspenders cross."

Murphy rocked a thumb at a paper tacked to the back-bar. "And now it's Shaniko that's on the dodge. Ridge brought that over a bit ago."

Wiley was coming in close, putting a palm on the bar and talking to the room at large with his face a foot from Tom's. An ugly push-and-pull was going on in his eyes.

"What I don't savvy," he said, "is when they passed a law against killing killers."

"The law," Tom said, "is against killing anybody with his hands in his pockets. Shaniko could have brought him in."

"A man would look good bringing in a maniac like McAllister, wouldn't he?"

"He doesn't look good gunning him down in cold blood," Tom said. "A man doesn't even look good priming an idiot with whiskey on an Indian reservation."

"Who's this you're talking about?" Wiley asked.

"According to what I heard Chunk say," Tom told him, "I'm talking about you."

He knew it would come, and he waited for it, braced, conscious of how swiftly the whole room had been caught up in a grudge that was the personal property of Carmody and Morg Wiley. But Wiley, dropping his hand to his side, made his fists and stood back.

"When did this town start swearing out warrants on the strength of your kind of say-so?" he demanded. "A Spik—and a four-flusher."

"I don't four-flush," Tom said. "I don't make any kind of brag often, but the one I made when I left here I've proved up on. Bannerman's out—Carmody's in. You aren't saying much about getting McAllister drunk, Morg," he smiled. "Aren't you going to call me a liar?"

"I didn't think I had to call you that," Wiley said. "I thought you ought to know it."

Tom watched him turn away. Then Wiley's sloping shoulders moved and he had turned swiftly, his left fist slashing up at Tom's jaw, his face twisted. He was a large and powerful man bent on smashing Tom to the floor.

Tom struck down at his forearm and hammered it aside, so that Wiley's knuckles hit the bar. Then his mouth hardened and he slashed at the point of the ramrod's chin.

Wiley's head was turned. Tom loved the solid bite of his knuckles. Wiley stumbled aside and went to his knees. He rested there a moment, giving his head a shake. His hand wiped blood from his lip and he looked up at Tom, and then the memory of fury flooded into his eyes and he pushed himself up with a palm against the floor. He came in with a roundhouse swing which knocked Tom's hat off. A Cross Anchor man yelled.

Tom fell away, his head humming. Wiley lunged in— huge, powerful, cumbersome. He swung and missed, stabbed and was short, and Tom kept backing. Wiley angrily reached for his shoulders with both hands, crazy with impatience.

But Tom was not running now; he was settling his boots on the earth floor, a cool satisfaction in his eyes, for Wiley was wide open, unguarded and off-balance, and Tom measured him as he would have measured a calf for a throw. Wiley saw him smile and heard him say the soft, taunting word, and he turned his head away, wincing.

The fist smashed into the side of his jaw, a right with all the power of Tom's back in it. Wiley's head shook, he staggered and tried to cover his face against the left Tom was driving in. As he struck, Tom let his fist tilt down; there was a straight line of bone and tendon between the edge of his fist and his shoulder when he hit. Wiley fell against the bar, turned and took one step into the room. He fell across a table and lay on his back on the floor with one arm moving slightly.

Someone was pounding Tom on the back. Murphy was saying, ''I'll set up a round myself, for that!'' But Tom was looking down at Wiley and wondering, *Is it always going to be this way?* The brief and savage clash he had anticipated so long had come and gone, and he felt nothing but pity for the ramrod and the empty knowledge that with a man like Wiley, this was not an end, but a beginning.

. . . He got Tig started after another round of drinks. The old man was charged with enthusiasm as they walked

upstreet. Tom let him talk. . . . On the mesa the wind
would be full and strong, whetted on the Rockies. Clance
Harper and Creed Davis would he keeping the herd bunched
for the daybreak drive. He could ride up tonight and join
them, with the news that the drive would not end until they
crossed Crooked River on the Snaketrack.

The scheming on paper had ended.

They went up the dark, drafty tunnel to the Cincinnatus
apartment. Laura answered Tom's knock. Seeing the curious look in her eyes, he wondered if he had taken a cut in
the fight with Wiley which he had not known about. She
was regarding him oddly. She said, "Tom, I—I think—"
Then he looked past her and saw the man sitting on the
horsehair sofa across the room. The man nodded at him
and faintly smiled.

. . . Laura said hastily, "Tig, there's quite a bit of
work to do before we need your signature, after all. Part of
the instrument has to be re-drawn. Why don't you go
along to the restaurant and have a bit to eat?"

"Now. Godamighty—!" Tig piped, but Tom turned and
said quickly:

"Go on back to the saloon. I'll bring the paper, ink, and
the judge down in fifteen minutes, and we'll sign it in
front of the whole town."

He pushed a little, to help Tig decide—fearful that he
would see the man in the parlor. And Tig swore and
shambled back down the stairs and slammed the lower
door.

Then Tom turned and entered the room, extending his
hand to the small, bearded, rifle-straight Mexican standing
on the red Indian rug. He said, "*Que hubole*, General?
I've been expecting you. Pete Trinidad told me you were
coming. . . ."

—19—

CINCINNATUS CAME INTO the room. He wore a ragged bathrobe the color of a grulla horse; he looked pallid and rumpled and worried, and he was making his pipe rattle the way he did when trouble had him backed to the wall. Laura went to make coffee and the general spoke after her with a politely imperious smile.

"*Muy oscuro,* if you please, señorita. Very dark."

Tom saw her chin tilt a bit as she went out. The general turned to him, then. They sat at opposite ends of the cracked leather sofa, Cincinnatus in his old green Morris chair. Lopez-Montezuma was dressed plainly in a brown suit and black boots spiked with Amozoc spurs.

"I hope you have expected me with pleasure, amigo?"

"Why not?" Tom said.

Lopez-Montezuma lifted one shoulder. A small man, he looked direct and alert. His skin was Indian-dark, his beard cut like General Grant's. There was kindness in him, Tom recalled, but it was kept in its place, for he was also a zealot, and being a zealot his gaze was fixed above the misery of those nearest him in wanting to relieve those far off. He had the vigor of an animal; he kept three mistresses and a dozen fine horses, the horses stolen here and there, the mistresses acquired as spoils of war and from other officers.

The Mexican told Tom he had been told by Marshal Ridge to look for him here. He had arrived in town a half-hour ago. "I am traveling with a few friends, who are camped back in the foothills," he explained.

"Army friends?" Tom asked.

"Well, who can say? It may develop into an army if I can raise enough money. It took all I had to escape the firing squad."

Tom asked about his escape, and at this point Laura brought coffee, but the general's was the same clear brown as the rest. It was Laura's answer to imperiousness. She sat down between him and Tom.

Lopez-Montezuma stirred the coffee and spoke vaguely of bribe, and night rides, and proudly of hiding in peasants' *jacales*. He mentioned a small nucleus of partisans in the mountains of Chihuahua or Sonora, he had forgotten which.

"And now," Tom said, "you want your money back."

"Certainly," the Mexican said.

"Well, I haven't got it," Tom said. And he looked at Cincinnatus.

Lopez-Montezuma crossed his legs the other way. "But you have properties, eh? Which can be sold?"

"Not overnight, my friend," Cincinnatus growled.

"Anything can be sold overnight."

"All right!" Cincinnatus snapped. "If you want to take ten cents on the dollar at forced sale, we'll sell it."

Lopez-Montezuma's anger was tempered. "Well, of course there is not so much haste as that—"

Tom kept his eyes on the judge, hoping he would go on, that he had the bare bones of some scheme in his head. But what scheme could there be, other than Tom's giving back what was not his?

Cincinnatus looked straight at Tom as he said, "No, there is never so much haste that a man cannot go carefully. How much," he asked, "do you figure Tom owes you?"

"At the present rate of exchange," said the general, "he would owe me twenty-eight thousand, five hundred dollars."

"What about the old rate of exchange?" the judge asked.

"Within a hundred dollars of the same," Lopez-Montezuma smiled.

"I see." Cincinnatus massaged his eyeballs with his fingers. "Well, we've got to work something out. Something that doesn't involve ruin for my client."

In a clear, hard voice, the Mexican stated, "There is nothing to be worked out but cash."

Tom's anger whipped up. "You forget, General—if I hadn't banked the money in El Paso for you, you wouldn't have anything now."

"At the moment," retorted the Mexican, "I haven't."

Laura spoke up tartly. "If you'd listen to my father, perhaps you'd get all of your money—sooner or later."

His polished black eyes snapping, the general regarded the judge steadily. After a moment Cincinnatus asked:

"What's the state of your finances at the moment, Tom?"

It was all in Tom's head—the only kind of books he knew how to keep. "I had three thousand of my own and I got twenty-eight when I changed the Mex gold into American. I spent ten on shorthorns and another thousand on range cattle. That's eleven. The lease is seventy-two hundred and I'll need six thousand to operate on til I've got a crop. . . . What's that total?"

"Twenty-four thousand, two hundred dollars," Laura said, promptly. "From thirty-one, is about seven thousand dollars."

"Seven thousand left," the Mexican said grimly, and rose quickly, setting down his coffee. He crossed the room and turned back, a dark shadow against the tawny wall. "Seven thousand is not enough."

"We're not asking you to take seven," Cincinnatus snapped. "Here's what I *am* asking: We can raise six or seven thousand on Tom's cattle, another five on the crop he's going to raise. Put the remaining cash with it, and you can leave here with seventeen thousand dollars, and Tom still in business. Next year he can rake up the rest."

"No," the General said.

Tom rose angrily. "General," he said, "I played square with you, where a lot of men wouldn't have. A lot of them would call the marshal right now, and that might be the end of your plans. But all I'm asking is that you play square with me, this time."

"I consider that I play square when I do not have you killed. A lot of men would do that, too."

He walked back, finished his coffee, and took a black round-crowned sombrero from the antelope prongs on the wall. "*'Ueno, señores, senorita. Es de*—a matter of time," he shrugged. "I give you one week to raise the money. You comprehend that I require it quickly for commitments of my own."

Tom said, "Yeah. I comprehend." He watched the general don a black shortcoat, remembering with a sort of homesickness how he had sat all night with him in smoky cafes, talking strategy, horses, and women. He smiled, then.

"I told you once to look me up if you were ever in the States. This isn't exactly the kind of party I planned, but— I'm still buying the drinks. The Great Western isn't much, but there are locks on the doors. I'll walk over with you and get you fixed up with a room."

Lopez-Montezuma smiled, the rancor vanishing from his face. "Still my *buen' hombre*. No—I have slept so long in the field that I can no longer sleep in a cage. Perhaps another time, when you are *gran' hacendado*, and I am president of Mexico, and neither of us is afraid of dying in his sleep."

From the door he tipped his hat to Laura. The lock clicked behind him.

In the quiet, Tom said, "A nice fella. I knew him in Mexico."

Cincinnatus leaned back in the deep armchair. He was gray and tired. "What are you going to do about him?"

"Pay up," Tom said. "What else can I do? It's his money."

Then he discovered Laura's gaze on him—she was smiling. She looked proud, he thought, and almost happy. "What did you think he'd do?" she asked her father.

"The way he's been carrying on, it's about what I'd expect him to do. Jump right out with both feet, the way he jumped in. Or he could take my advice and give some more thought to it.''

''There doesn't seem to be much to think about,'' Tom said.

Rising, Cincinnatus went to the door of his bedroom. He hesitated, and spoke without turning back. ''Frankly,'' he said, ''there doesn't. But we've got a day or two before we have to start liquidating. We'll make it count.''

The door closed, the parlor was silent, and Laura regarded Tom, her fingers playing with the chatelaine watch. The grayness in him was like a chill. He stared at the gray-red pattern of the hearth, expressionless.

''What are you thinking?'' Laura asked.

''I'm thinking,'' he said, ''that you were right. I didn't come back to make a success. I came back to throw it in Bannerman's face. Losing the money is tough. But what I'm really sorry about is that it may be years before I can take another crack at him. And that's what I want most of all. I want to wipe his face in the range he's lorded so long. I want to wreck him; but I've never been farther from it than I am tonight.''

Her face had changed when he looked up. It was as though she had withdrawn from him. She looked at him now like a stranger.

''You've got a strange code, Tom. You'll play fairly with everyone but yourself. You'll go broke to pay back a rebel. But all you want for yourself is unhappiness for someone else. Do you think that's the same as finding happiness for yourself?''

''I don't know,'' Tom said. ''But I'm going to find out. . . .''

—20—

THIS DAY, THIS NIGHT—Tom Carmody would never forget them. A day that started with murder and ended with ruin. In a box in the shed of Fleming, the undertaker, lay Chunk McAllister, not a pulse less dead than Tom's dream of a cattle empire. This year had been written in chalk and rubbed out. He stood where he had when he left Soledad, possessor of the smallest ranch and the biggest hate in Union County.

He had seen men devoured by hate, eaten up by it while it hunted an outlet. It would not be that way with him: Laura was wrong. If he could not take Snaketrack away from Bannerman, he would get at him another way.

Cincinnatus had said he would not give up. But what could he do? A man who had cheated the firing-squad wanted his money. That was that.

He went to the hotel, but Trinidad had left. His hat, his gun, were missing. And Tom's mouth broke with a crooked grin. You too! Trinidad with his dead dream of killing Jim Shaniko. Limping about hunting a man who would be fifty miles away.

He looked at himself in the mirror. He looked solemn and hungry and accusative. He rubbed the stubble of whiskers on his jaw. But the hardness he saw went deeper than whiskers. It went clear into him. He puffed out the flame with a mouthful of cigarette smoke.

When he left the hotel, the desk clerk told him Ruth Bannerman had been looking for him. "Tell her I'll be back, if she comes again," Tom said.

But he had walked only a short distance when he saw her crossing the street. She stepped mincingly on the frozen ruts, holding her skirts high, the wind whipping at them. Tom stood there with anger stirring dully in him, remembering how she had decoyed him out of town the other night to give her father free rein with Tignal Jones. She waved at him, and he went to her. She took his arm in relief.

"Thank heaven! I thought I'd have to stay out here till the thaw!"

"I ought to leave you here till you freeze," Tom said.

Ruth was silent until they reached the boardwalk. "Tom, I know what you mean. But it's not true. I asked you to ride with me because I wanted to talk."

Tom tried to see into her motives, now, but she had a better poker face than any man he knew. He said, "The clerk was saying you were looking for me. Who sent you this time?"

"I'm on my own—as I was before. And when you've heard me, you'll believe it. Something's happened that you ought to know about."

He waited, quizzically, but she shook her head. "Not that I'm afraid of Dad," she said, "but it might antagonize him less if we talked on a side street. You see, I threw over Morg today."

"That ought to make your father happy. He wouldn't have had Morg as a son-in-law if he were gold-plated, would he?"

She thought an instant. "I'm not sure. I've always thought the man didn't live who'd satisfy Dad. Not that he cared particularly whether I liked him myself," she added. "Just that he had to be proper timber for a cattle baron. But Morg's played his cards wiser than I ever thought he could. He's finally got Dad thinking that a plodding son-in-law he could control would be better than an imaginative one he couldn't! Every now and then Dad will say something about Morg that tells me he's trying to talk both of us into it."

Then she smiled smugly and said, "But after what I told

Morg today, I don't think either of them will have any delusions about the crown passing to a Wiley!"

Tom chuckled. As they passed the hotel, his attention was caught by a ruby glow on the porch. He had a swift need to flinch, but held himself stiffly until he knew that the man in the cane chair was Pete Trinidad.

"How's the leg, Pete?" he called.

"Thought I'd stretch it. People die in bed, you know."

"They die on hotel porches, too."

They reached an alley between two buildings. Tom hesitated, glancing down the dark slot with its gleams of frozen mud. The wind thrust strongly through it. Ruth laughed softly.

"Why, Tom! There's no one you're afraid of, is there?"

"In front of me, no. In back of me, yes."

They went through to a narrow, treeless side street where the wind came with a clean rush against them. "I heard about your money coming up," Ruth said. "I suppose it would sound disloyal to say I'm glad, but—I am. Dad's had success. Why shouldn't someone else have a chance at it?"

"Just what I was telling my cowpunchers this afternoon."

"I heard about Chunk McAllister, too," she said, with a note of chiding in her voice. "Tom, I think you have a little list somewhere. Morg's name was on it, and you whipped him. Shaniko's, too. I wonder if he'll get the same as Chunk."

"Well, who gave it to Chunk?"

Her face was thoughtful. "I wonder—! No one seems to be sure. I heard something else, too. Shaniko's horse was found in a thicket by the river. It was a half-mile below town."

Tom's spurs chimed dully as they walked. "I wish you'd told me before. I'd have sent Trinidad inside."

"Tom—" Ruth said, "is my father's name on your list, too?"

"Is my name on your father's?"

She was silent a moment. "Yes," she said, "it's right at the top. He told me he won't quit until he's run you out.

He'll break you, he said, into pieces so small you'll never put them together again.''

"Even now that I've got Snaketrack?"

"You've only got it for five years, he says, and maybe he can do something about that. He's a fighter, Tom, and he's only started to fight."

"That's what you wanted to tell me?" Tom asked.

They turned a corner. "No. I wanted to tell you how you can beat him."

"I know how I'm going to beat him. The same way I beat Wiley. Block his swings and land my own."

Ruth sighed. "God gave men strong bodies, but He gave women imagination. Tom, dear, can't you see it? We don't have to govern ourselves by what Dad will or might do. If we went ahead with what he stopped last time, *he'd* be stopped. Because I'm of age, now, and there's nothing he could do. Besides, he wouldn't go to war with me, and he couldn't fight you without fighting me! Don't you see it?"

"I see him coming after us with a thirty-thirty again," Tom said. But a train of thought was started in him—if he really wanted to get at Bannerman, the way was through Ruth! The notion burned out in an instant, and he looked at her more clearly than he ever had, and saw her fully.

"In other words," he said, "I might not be much of a catch, but I'd sure make your father miserable."

Ruth exclaimed in annoyance. "Must you always pretend not to understand me? Tom, you know that if I didn't love you, I wouldn't marry you if you were the biggest rancher in New Mexico."

"On the other hand, would you have me if I were the smallest?"

"I don't know. I've been used to things so long that perhaps I couldn't be happy without them." She looked at him quickly, with a sparkle in her eyes. "Why don't you face it, Tom—you still love me, but you're afraid of Dad. Isn't that it?"

"No," Tom said. "I don't think either of us is in love."

They turned a corner onto Front Street again, but Ruth

Frank Bonham

held back. "Tom, let's not spoil everything! If we leave it this way, we're both too proud to give in. There's every reason why we shouldn't be frightened out now."

"And one or two why we should."

Her eyes inspected him critically; then she laughed softly. "I know what's wrong with you—you're superstitious. You think that there's a cloud over us because of the way it went last time."

"Maybe I do," Tom admitted.

"All right," she said. "I'm going to prove you're wrong. Tonight I'm going out to the ranch. I'm going to pack a suitcase and drive over to your cabin. We'll catch the train to Santa Fe from Agency siding tomorrow afternoon. Oh, as properly as though we had a duenna!" she said. "In two weeks, away from the things that spoil it here, we'll find it again—as exciting as ever."

Tom piloted her along the walk. "Or we'd find ourselves bickering in two days' time."

"Wouldn't it be worthwhile to find that out, even?"

Tom shrugged.

Nearing the hotel, he noticed a salt of fine snow in the air, a sift of crystals. A side door of Bailey's Livery Stable squalled on a rusted hinge and some men came out. They were abreast of Tom and Ruth, across the road, and he tried to make them out—and then he knew, and stopped.

One of the men was Jim Shaniko.

"Wait a minute, Ruth," he said, moving her toward the deep bay of a store-front.

Then he knew that she had seen them, too. "No, Tom! That's Dad and Morg with him. They're taking him in. Let it go at that."

"With Trinidad on the hotel porch?"

He walked swiftly along the boardwalk, the empty street between him and the trio hurrying along. He tried to see the front of the hotel, but it was blocked by the large sign of the saloon, creaking in the wind. He stepped off the walk for a better look at it. Then he saw the man at the top of the steps—a lean and dangerous shape with a high-crowned Mexican hat.

130

Tom's shout split the dark street. "Bannerman! Take him back to the stable."

Bannerman turned. Morgan Wiley hunched against the wall, his hand at his hip, and Tom shouted again, "Take him back!" Then he turned toward the hotel. "Pete, you crazy *pelado!* Get inside!"

Shaniko broke and ran, sliding swiftly along the wall toward the far corner. He was across from the saloon. Then he was past it, and a voice light with exultation called:

"Hold it up, Señor Deputy! Taking you in."

—21—

Shaniko swerved against a broken-plastered wall, one palm slapping his side, the other pressing against the wall. Trinidad stood straight.

"The hands high, amigo! *Aprisa!*"

Shaniko's Colt was out, firing prematurely. The first bullet chiseled into the frozen street. The second struck the wooden railing of the hotel. The third bullet was from Pete Trinidad's gun, missing Shaniko and hitting the wall beside him.

Bannerman and Wiley had their guns out and Tom saw them throwing down on the Mexican. *I told you, Pete!* he thought. And now there was no way in the world he could help him.

Thrown high by the kick of the revolver, Trinidad's hand descended slowly. Another shot roared from Shaniko's Colt. The shallow canyon of the street was filled with the clamor of gunfire. And Carmody heard Trinidad's voice in a lonesome cabin . . .

I'm going to be standing on the porch of the Great Western, and he's going to be coming out of Brophy's. . . .

Trinidad hadn't missed it far.

Tom heard the deputy's shot strike the adobe hotel wall solidly. Plaster fell. Trinidad's gun jumped again, the orange lick of its muzzle slashing past the porch railing. When the echoing blast stilled, Tom saw Shaniko falling forward. He heard the Mexican's gun explode again. Shaniko cried out and stumbled into the street. He fell on his face.

Bannerman's revolver roared hugely, and Tom winced.

But Trinidad was gone. He had backed through the open door of the hotel. There were shouts from the saloon and the hotel lobby, and inside the hotel the light fell into blackness.

Tom took three steps to a foot-path between two buildings. He came out on the back alley. Turning, he ran to the back of the hotel. There was a horse here, and he stood by it until suddenly a screen door creaked and someone limped from the hotel. Trinidad's gun was still in his hand. Tom spoke quickly.

"Pete, you crazy Mex! What've you done?"

Trinidad uttered a rattle of *cholo*. "Whatever I've done, it was worth it! Don't try to stop me, Tomas. In a week, he'd 'a' been out of jail, and I'd 'a' been in."

"No, Pete. He'd've stayed in."

"Okay, Tomas, he'd have stayed in. But me, I'm going to stay out—out of Soledad, New Mexico. Out of the States, maybe. Give me the reins!"

Men were shouting in the street and in the hotel. Trinidad was sobbing with excitement. His right hand clutched his injured leg. "Get out of my way! I won't go back to that rock *cimenterio* in Santa Fe—and they ain't going to hang me here."

"No, Pete. They may reward you. Shaniko was on the dodge. Hit for the mesa and tell Creed and Clance to start the herd for my place tonight. You move with them. If you see anybody coming, slope for the trees, but stay where we can find you. We'll have you clear in twenty-four hours."

Trinidad's hand clutched his arm. "If you trick me—"

"You're on my payroll, aren't you? Any cowman worth a damn will back up his men."

The Mexican was gone, riding through the stiff weeds, losing himself in the darkness. . . .

There was a group of women at the entrance to the alley when Tom cut back. He saw Ruth among them and steered her down the street. Lanterns winked like fireflies. A huddle of men had collected where Shaniko lay. At the corner, lamps burned in Cincinnatus' windows and Tom thought of Laura, and wished he were with her—he wished it with a sudden desire that hurt. You could want a woman because she stimulated you, or because she was sane when everyone else was crazy. This town was crazy. He was crazy and Bannerman was crazy and everyone else was crazy. But Laura would be sane. She would talk sanity and no one would listen to her—not even Tom Carmody, because he didn't dare.

Ruth's voice was tense. "He killed Shaniko! He shot him down."

"And Shaniko killed McAllister. That's an even trade."

He left her and crossed the street.

Marshal Ridge had come in vest and shirtsleeves. He was shivering with cold. "Do we have to stand out here and freeze?" he said. "Where the devil's the doctor?"

Bannerman's voice said, "Let's move into Brophy's. Morg, stay with Jim."

Then he saw Carmody and gave him a long, dry stare. He turned away, put a hand on the marshal's shoulder and walked with him to the saloon, like a man sharing trouble with a friend.

Brophy had not done such business in six months. His little saloon was crowded. Every man had a drink in his hand, except the men who were being careful and wanted to think straight. Tom was not drinking, Bannerman was not drinking, Marshal Ridge was dry and unhappy. With a piece of cue-chalk, he drew a line on a pool table.

"This here's the street," he stated. "Now, call this the stable—"

"To hell with diagrams!" snapped Bannerman. "Has anything been done about catching that Spik?"

"I've got a dozen boys going through alleys and back lots. He can't squirm out without a horse, and if he's riding he'll be seen."

Bannerman's hand held a pool-ball. He gave it a sudden swipe so that it struck a side cushion and thudded on the floor. "Here's *my* diagram!" he stated. "Five hundred dollars for the man who brings in Pete Trinidad, dead or alive!

"On what charge?" Tom asked.

Bannerman was holding himself down. He stared at

Tom. He said, "Murder. Shaniko was in custody when the Mexican threw down on him."

Ridge's voice had a bite. "Pete never threw down on him. I get it that he told him to put his hands up. Shaniko threw down an Pete—he fired the first shot. If his conscience was clear, why did he hide his horse in a thicket and sneak into town after dark?"

"My God!" Bannerman shouted. *"The man had been bush-whacked!* He went out to take a murderer, and he was fired on from the bushes. Would you expect him to come riding down Front Street in front of a brass band? I'll pay five hundred dollars," he said to the room at large, "to the man who brings Trinidad in."

"Before there can be a reward," Ridge stated, "there has to be a warrant. I find no cause for issuing a warrant for Trinidad. As far as I'm concerned, Shaniko was trying to escape justice, Trinidad shot him in self-defense."

Tom had not heard Morgan Wiley come in. But now he saw the Cross Anchor ramrod behind the marshal. And he heard Wiley's rough voice in the quiet.

"What happened out there at that line-camp? That's what *I* want to know." He was looking at Tom, the scars of their fight plain on his face.

"That's all down on my blotter," Ridge snapped.

"It ain't down over the signature of a coroner's jury. We've got the word of a man Carmody'd fought with, and an exconvict, that Shaniko shot McAllister. How the hell do we know *they* didn't do it?"

With the blue cue-chalk, Ridge made a large X on the pool table. "All right. If you want to put the taxpayers to the expense of a coroner's jury, we'll call one. In the meantime, anybody who molests the Mexican will answer to me."

Bannerman's mouth eased. "I'll go along with that. But I'll expect you to go along with this: Carmody stays off Snaketrack until this is settled."

"Why should I?" Tom demanded.

"Why should you? For the same reason a panhandler with fifty thousand dollars in his pocket shouldn't have the use of it until he's proved up on it."

"I've proved up on this. I'll put my cattle on when I'm ready. That may be tomorrow or a week from tomorrow."

Bannerman spoke across the table. His eyes had a gaunt and acid look, a look more bitter than Tom had ever seen. "No, you won't," he said. "You won't put one cow on that land before this is settled. Ridge," he said, "will you back that up?"

Ridge shook his head. "No."

"Then I will. I'll regard that land as quarantined until it's been proved otherwise. I don't mean by a check. I mean by proving to me that Carmody didn't kill McAllister and saddle my man with it."

He threw the cold cigar on the table and left the saloon.

Afterward, Tom and Ridge had a drink without words. They went into the night. Ridge looked mournfully along the street, and said, "This was a good little town. A hell of a good little town."

"No," Tom said. "It just seemed good. Underneath, a lot of people have always been boiling."

Ridge's smile was one-sided. "You're fooling somebody if you think this fight is over how big Bannerman is. It's because you were in love with Ruth, once, and he made an ass of you. Listen, Tom! You don't even love her any more. Why go to war over her?"

"I don't aim to," Tom smiled.

"That's good!" Ridge sounded enthusiastic, but his eyes were suddenly curious. "Then there's—nobody right now?"

Tom lifted his shoulders, smiling. *"Quien sabe?"* he said.

The marshal, unexpectedly warmed, laying a hand on Tom's arm. "I'm going to tell you something, son. Find somebody! You'll need a woman out there. It'll be lonesome, and there's a-many chores a man ain't fit for. You'll need a cook and housekeeper, somebody to keep the place from turning into a bunkhouse. And of course," he added solemnly, "love ain't to be overlooked, either. It's a bigger influence in a man's life than you might think."

Tom stared at him. This correct, middle-aged lawman

with old dodgers for guts and handcuffs for a heart—telling him about love! "Oh, it's a big influence, all right," he agreed. "So you got tired of baching and decided on a wife eh?"

Ridge winced. "That boarding house! God damn. If I ever hated anything, it's dried-apple pies and that widow woman's got a shed full of dried apples. Well, one night the judge had me over on business and Laura had green-apple pie. . . . Lordy, Tom, I'd never looked at her before. I looked then. And it started." He struck his heart twice with his fist. "Forty-five years a bachelor, and then—" he chuckled.

"Mike, I want you to do me a favor," Tom said earnestly. "She loves you. Don't ever spoil it by telling her you're marrying her to get out of a boarding house."

"Why, shoot, Tom—!" Ridge began, but Tom was walking away from him into the darkness.

—22—

By TWO O'CLOCK the town had become utterly silent. A light snow was falling. Now and then from the hotel room, Tom looked down on the dark street, ghostly under the snow. He smoked cigars until the taste of them sickened him. From Trinidad's half-finished bottle, he took a mouthful of whiskey.

He sat again on the edge of the bed with a newspaper folded over his knees and a sheet of writing paper upon it, and inscribed once more the figures of catastrophe. In an agony of frustration he hurled the paper at the wall and blew out the lamp. He pulled off his boots and lay under the heavy quilted comforter.

. . .Chunk McAllister moved across the room, showing him the holes in his breast from Shaniko's bullets. And Shaniko made his silent complaint against bad luck and fate, justifying himself. Tom did not hate him any more, he despised him for a liar and a coward—but he did not hate him. He remembered how he had felt when he saw Morgan Wiley lying on the floor. How he had pitied him, and wished there were a better way to settle things than this.

How else? He had tried Laura's slow-and-easy way before. It had backed him into an alley of the mountains. The last time he looked out the window the snow had stopped. The stars were hard and white. He wondered whether Ruth was foolish enough to go to the cabin to wait for him . . .

While he was eating breakfast, a rain started; in a short

time the snow was gone. The rain drew back to the mountains; an iron cold took the town in its fist.

Walking to the judge's, he had the feeling that he was gesticulating on a stage from which the rest of the actors had departed. The play was over, but he must walk up and down until Cincinnatus said it could end. Cincinnatus was rambling around the parlor in his threadbare robe. "Sit down, Tom!" he commanded. "Laura, get him some coffee. Put some brandy in it."

Tom watched her move to the kitchen and return with coffee and a pint of brandy. Her movements were collected, graceful; she was neat from the part of her hair to the hem of her gown. She was independent, calm—completely a woman, and the man to whom she gave herself could wear her like a diamond-studded watch seal.

Did the man have to be a ludicrous town marshal who wanted a young wife and some home cooking? He peered yearningly into her face, and knew it would not be Tom Carmody, whether Ridge got her or not. She had withdrawn herself from him.

Cincinnatus began to thump his knees with his fist. "Damn it, Tom, why should I care what happens to you? You got yourself into this mess. Not one blessed thing has happened that I didn't expect to happen."

There was a silence. "Lopez-Montezuma was here this morning," Laura said. "Did you say he'd been a friend of yours? He wasn't talking like it."

The judge's glance was on Tom, full of melancholy. "Do you want to quit, Tom? I don't see a hole for you to wriggle out of, except to tell him to go to hell. And if you do, you'll be at war with Mexico as well as Bannerman."

Tom poured brandy into the coffee. "No. I'll finish it out. . . . I could sell most of my cattle," he said, "and bring it up pretty close."

"And use what for a herd?"

Tom shrugged. Finishing the coffee, he stood up to go. "I may ride out to the ranch today to see about the cattle. Take it easy."

"We aren't giving up," Cincinnatus tried to summon cheer. "There's one other matter. . . . Well, why get you worked up? We'll know by tonight whether there's any-thing to it.''

Laura went onto the landing with him. She hugged herself with the cold, but looked at Tom very intently, with sympathy.

"Tom, I want to be sure you understand me. You know how I've always felt about you. I know you can't help the way you are, but it scares me, just the same. A man who puts vengeance above everything else . . . there's no end to it, is there? It isn't enough to build a life on. When you've beaten Bannerman to his knees, what comes next?''

"Then I can build for myself," Tom said.

"But you're supposed to be building for yourself now! And yet you want to wreck him even more than you want to do these things for Tom Carmody! You claim that Bannerman is mean and hard—but even he didn't put a foundation of vengeance under himself. Can't you see that?''

"All I can see," he sighed, "is that Bannerman has been the thumb over me for the last ten years. And now he's going back on Snaketrack, and I'm out, but if he lets his guard down just once—!'' He closed his fist. "I've got to wind this up,'' he said. "Laura, this is something I've got to finish before I can go anywhere.''

She smiled, with warmth, with understanding, but with pity. "Then good luck, Tom.''

"And goodbye, eh?'' Tom smiled.

"No, I like Pete's words better—'Vaya con dios!' That's what I really mean.''

He stood in the wintry street. He thought of his men trying to bed a breachy gang of cows on insufficient range, and suddenly he wanted to be with them, doing something clearcut and understandable. He walked briskly to Bailey's and got his chestnut from a stall while Bailey sucked a straw and watched him slip the bit in the gelding's mouth.

"Seems like you got 'em *all* on the run!'' Bailey re-marked. "Ruth Bannerman took off in her buggy last night and about sunup Morg Wiley was rousting me out for his pony. Then a half-hour ago Bannerman took out on his bay, looking sore enough to eat boiled sheep. Reckon they're wanting to be shut of this town, now it ain't Bannerman-ville any more!"

Tom hesitated before he pulled on the latigo. Ruth had gone out last night. . . . Where? To pack, as she had said she would, and go on to his cabin? Slowly he drew on the leather.

"Bannerman say where he was going?" he asked.

"Does that 'un ever say where he's going?"

For a moment he sat the horse before the barn. A weary wet crew of cowpunchers were taking a small herd of cattle into the station. Over every chimney in town hung a flattened mushroom of smoke. Shreds of snow lingered under the piñons. It was a bleak picture, but nostalgic, and he thought, *I almost owned this town, once.* . . . And what was to keep him here, now? Let Ridge have Laura, let Bannerman have Snaketrack, for those things were settled, and let him have a trail leading out. But there was no lure beyond Soledad. There was left in him no young dream of another lucky coup like his rebel fortune.

A man came into sight suddenly on the corner. Tom recognized the bony frame of Marshal Ridge. Ridge stood there looking downstreet and all at once raised a yellow-gloved hand. He strode along the walk, and Tom turned the pony into the street and stopped at a frozen horse-trough to meet him. Half of Ridge's face was shaved; the other half was still stubbed, and the yellow Buffalo Bill mustache was untrimmed. At once Tom saw the shine of anxiety in him.

"Tom! Where's your cattle?" Ridge demanded.

"On the trail," Tom said.

"Got the lease buttoned up?"

"As good as," Tom said.

Ridge snapped, "Nothing's as-good-as! Why don't you kill that business off?"

"Not ready," Tom said.

Ridge clamped his jaws in exasperation. "I don't know how crazy Bannerman can get, but Murphy came down just now to tell me something Wiley'd said in the saloon last night. He claimed he had Bannerman's okay to stop

141

you from using the land, and he aimed to do it. Well, maybe that was whiskey-talk. But remember what Bannerman told you after Shaniko was killed! And this morning Murphy seen him and Bannerman both leaving town, a half-hour apart, and he got to ponderin' on it. And now he's got *me* ponderin'. Because somebody seen your cows moving south last night and Bannerman shore knows it if anybody does!''

. . . Suddenly Tom was breathless.

This isn't over cows, Mike—this is over Ruth! Wiley's told him she threw him over. And he thinks she's gone out to run off with me again. Tom had wanted a way to get at him, and this was it. Even Bannerman, the shrewd and long-thinking, could be carried away by a rage too great to contain. He was doing the thing that Tom, if he had been given the privilege of planning the rancher's strategy, would have instructed him to do. He was acting rashly and beyond the law. He was planning to vent his fury on Tom's men and cattle for something Ruth was doing. . . .

"I'm thinking about Harper," Ridge said. "He hates Bannerman's guts, and if Bannerman tries to stop the herd, there may be gunplay. And what if Trinidad is with them?"

"That's a thought, too," Tom said; and he grinned. "I'd better get out there, Mike. There's no need for you to come. He'll bluff out."

"He will like hell," Ridge bit out. "If he don't make trouble, you will. I'm going along to keep the peace, Tom. That means you as well as him."

"There won't be any trouble as far as I'm concerned," said Tom. "I'm not putting my cattle on Snaketrack until I'm ready."

"Just the same, I'm going with you. Drag along and wait for me. . . ."

—23—

THREADING THE FROSTY foothills, the cattle trail took the long and easy way to Tom's high-country ranch.

The scuffed trail of the Shorthorns was bared by the melting snow. Tom kept the pony at a stiff rack, hoping to outdistance Ridge. The hills sloughed away south and east; the wind came with a sting of ice. At the top of Johnson Grade, the marshal caught up with him.

"You drag along like six horses and a blacksnake!" he charged.

Tom rode on without comment.

He attempted to think with Bannerman's mind. Bannerman would find Ruth and—he winced. First she had coaxed him into deeding the hay ranch to her. She had played along with him and made a fool out of Wiley, and brought everything to Tom as a dowry. He could see Bannerman punishing her as he would a stubborn horse, and then coming back from the cabin to wait for Tom and the herd. . . .

He could not fit Wiley into it exactly. Having lost out, what would the ramrod do? He would play the cards Bannerman gave him. But he knew Wiley needed only a command and he would do as Chunk McAllister had done for Bannerman.

He was riding toward gunplay. And he was glad.

From high ground, they caught a glimpse of the dark bodies of the cattle on a hillside, winding down into a valley. Ridge seemed to relax.

"All right, so far!"

They were about a half-hour from the cabin at the head of the canyon where Crooked River made up. It would come soon, and Tom had a crying urge to shake the marshal. But he was silent while they worked up a long hogback through stairsteps of rimrock and bands of small timber. They emerged into the full sweep of the wind. The hillside fell away into a broad and shallow canyon. Drifts of brown leaves lay among the trees; cholla tangles and gaunt boulders made the descent trying. And down there, abruptly, Tom saw something that was not rock and was not cholla. . . .

He raised his arm to point at the far hillside. "Look yonder!"

Ridge shook his head. "I don't see anything."

"No, he's laying doggo, now. I saw a rifle shine."

Ridge's face tightened. "By God! Those damned fools!" His head turned and he looked down into the little valley, where Tom's herd was sluggishly coming up, driven by Clance Harper and Creed Davis and a dark horseman who could have been Trinidad.

Tom said through his teeth, "That's Trinidad, Mike! I sent him out to keep him away from the Cross Anchor crowd."

Ridge looked at him, his lips pressed together. He leaned closer, as if trying to pick up his line of sight. "I don't reckon Bannerman would bring his whole crew along. I don't think they'd do murder even for him."

"But Wiley would."

The marshal nodded. "Yes, Wiley would. Wiley'd murder those boys down there and slaughter half your herd, and sleep fine tonight. Here's something maybe you don't know about Wiley. Cincinnatus told me yesterday. He's been holding it, laying for him. Couple of years ago Wiley put an ad in an El Paso legal paper—one of them 'I-will-not-be-responsibile-for-debts-of-my-wife' things."

"Is Wiley married?" Tom exclaimed.

"Looks like it, though when the judge asked him about it he got sore and swore it was somebody else. Cincinnatus forgot it. But when Ruth came back and Wiley primed Chunk to raising hell, he got to thinking that Wiley might be afraid he'd keep him from marrying her. So you can see Wiley ain't to be messed with. But, Tom—" he said. "I don't see Bannerman in this!"

"Wait ten minutes. Maybe you'll see him then."

Ridge studied. "Maybe Wiley and him ain't even together. They left town separately, you know. Tom," he asked, "is there any reason he might think you and Ruth were planning to run off together?"

Tom stared down the slope; he saw a patch of horsehide move among pinking boulders. *"Quien sabe?* He's suspicious enough for three men. But if that was a gunman I saw across the canyon, those boys of mine are going to ride into a crossfire while we sit here. You can ride down to the toe of this ridge without being seen. Then cut to the other side. If you follow the men over there, and I take this side, there won't be much shooting."

Ridge's grim eyes checked Tom's strategy. He moved on the saddle. He watched the cowboys below unconcernedly swinging their ropes at stragglers. The sound of their how'ing them into line came with the bawling of the animals.

"I guess so," Ridge decided. "We'll try it." . . . He took Tom's glance sternly. "Now, listen! No gunplay unless they throw down on you. Savvy?"

"I got it," Tom grinned.

Walking down the slope, Tom kept his eyes where he had seen a man's horsehide jacket in the rocks near the bottom. He knew it was Morgan Wiley, but for a while he could not see him. In places, the dead leaves were a foot deep. He moved carefully, the Henry balanced across his hands. His whole body was clamped in an effort at stealth.

And he stopped and searched for Bannerman. Sending Ridge across the canyon had been merely to give himself a clear field. But now, seeing no evidence of the rancher nearby, he wondered if he had unwittingly guessed his strategy.

Presently he reached a flat table of rock jutting from the hillside. About a hundred feet below him lay the Cross Anchor ramrod. Wiley sprawled in a cairn of rocks, his carbine resting in a slot, his Stetson lying beside him. In the chill sunlight, his spurs had a cold glint.

Below him, Pete Trinidad threw a cigarette butt at an ambling steer and looked up the slope. His eye seemed to slide over Tom without seeing him. Wiley lay still. Trinidad gave his rope a twirl and jogged ahead. Wiley let him move out of range without raising the rifle. He lay there, stolidly waiting for the man who owned these cows, the man he must have thought would have joined his cowpunchers by now. . . .

At last he came up on his knees. He left his gun lying there. Then he pulled his fist back and drove it savagely against his palm, and Tom heard him swear. He knew with certainty, then, that Wiley had come out here to kill one man—he would not take even Pete Trinidad as second-best.

Tom knew, then, that when Wiley saw him, nothing in the world could keep him from firing.

Tom stood on the jut of rock, his shoulders sloping, the carbine ready. He watched Wiley observe the passing of the punchers. He saw him bend and pick up the rifle and turn north to study the canyon as if for a straggler. He turned upslope, then, to return to his horse, and at that instant he saw Tom. There was a shocked instant when he stood still. His face was walnut-dark, black-browed, blank. Then his features broke wildly, he went to his knees, and the rifle snapped up.

Tom yelled: *"Drop it, Morg!"*

Wiley threw the shot by instinct. The sound was an expansive, shaking roar, striking Tom almost like a fist. The bullet mashed itself on the rocks behind him and shrieked off through the trees.

Tom saw in the notched sights of his rifle how Wiley yanked the lever of his Winchester down and slammed it back into place; how he brought the gun up again with an expression of desperation. Then a gray smut of powder bloomed between them, as Tom's rifle bucked. His shoulder was jarred by the shot. He jacked up another shell. Across the canyon he heard the echoes coming back, carrying Marshal Ridge's shout with them.

He took a quick sidestep to throw Wiley off. But Wiley

had dropped his gun. It lay in the leaves at his feet. His chin had sagged to his breast and his arms hung deeply, and now his legs gave way. He fell huddled but rolled over on his back.

For a while Tom stared at him. Then he was aware that a half-mile away the marshal had left the trees and was riding across the valley toward them. He turned swiftly and strode back up the hill to his pony.

He knew where Bannerman would be, now. He was driven to find him, to let it all be finished. It was like a cold craziness in him. He was being stampeded into it, wanting to think it out first, yet compelled by a force within himself to rush ahead.

If Bannerman were not with Wiley, then they had not come out together. They had come independently—both driven to it by Ruth. Both looking for Tom Carmody, Wiley in the herd, Bannerman at the cabin.

Tom slanted a look down into the canyon, widening now into the meadow. Here at the lower end his cattle were being driven into the timber by three startled cowpunchers who brandished Colts and yelled at the cattle and each other. He had left Ridge and his shouting behind.

The shake-roofed cabin, the pole corrals and small barn, lay on the tawny meadow, pushed up against the timber. The sun was lemon-yellow, evoking wraiths of steam from the fence-rails, melting the tatters of snow in the yard and beneath the trees. Tom saw no horse in the corral, no sign of a buggy.

He scanned the greasy trail. No other horse had been over it recently. For a long time he sat his pony among the trees above the cabin. . . . A rider from Cross Anchor would cut over the saddle east of the cabin. A rider from town would be on the trail Tom had taken. After five minutes he jogged down to the meadow.

He passed the irrigation ditch he had dug for a kitchen garden, the unharvested rows of carrots and onions gone wildly to seed. He let his glance run on across the bare yard with its ricks of ironwood and rusting gear, to the broken porch of the cabin. He saw the girl who stood in the doorway.

"You damned little fool!" he breathed.

He was on the point of lifting his pony into a lope when he saw the horseman at his left, at the edge of the meadow just under the saddle. He saw this man throw a cigar to the ground and flick his horse with the rein-ends. Tom stared at him, glanced back at the doorway in cold alarm, and saw that Ruth had vanished into the cabin. He did not know whether Bannerman had seen her.

Bannerman carried a rifle across his saddle and he rode straight at Tom. Tom halted his horse. He held it with his knees and his hands squeezed the Henry. He waited.

Everything had focussed down with beautiful simplicity. It was utterly plain. Bannerman would say, *Is Ruth here?* And Tom would speak one word and watch, through Bannerman's eyes, the crumpling of something inside him. The man who had tried to control a daughter through arrogance, and then with kindness and gifts, would hear Tom Carmody say, "Yes. She's waiting for me."

He could see Bannerman's rigid features. He saw the hard set of his body as he came on. He thought, I'll soften him in a hurry! But with a kind of astonishment, as Bannerman rode up, he saw something more than anger in his eyes. He saw pain. It startled Tom. Bannerman's hard austerity was gone.

Bannerman turned his pony broadside to Tom's. His features were dark and twisted. "She's here, isn't she?" he shouted.

"Is she?" Tom said.

"She told Wiley she was going back to you. *Is she here!*" Bannerman demanded.

Tom started to speak, but set his lips. *What am I waiting for?* he wondered. He had lived a year for this. Was it what he saw in Bannerman's eyes that held him, or was it what Laura had been telling him ever since he came back? *A man who puts vengeance above everything else—there's no end to it, is there?*

Bannerman's hands managed the rifle as though they were merely waiting for a command. . . . He forced his voice down. But still that twist of pain in his features,

148

there were those creases of agony between his eyes; and Tom pitied him.

"I told you what I'd do to you if you tried to take her away from me," Bannerman said bitterly.

"Maybe I don't like being told," Tom said.

I'm stalling, he thought. Afraid to pull the trigger. I can kill this man—kill something more important to him than his body—and I'm afraid to do it.

Bannerman turned his head and scrutinized the cabin. He faced Tom again. He looked old and beaten. His voice was gray. He said, "You're afraid to answer me. Ruth's inside that cabin."

Well, Tom? Was it Laura's voice? *You came back for this, didn't you? . . . Are you afraid of how you felt after you killed Wiley? . . . Or—is it easier to kill than to mutilate?*

Suddenly there was a melting sensation in Tom. A cold core he had carried for a year was dissolving. And he heard someone saying, "No. I don't know where Ruth is, but she isn't here."

Bannerman's eyes challenged him. "You're lying!" he said.

Tom shrugged. "Look in the cabin."

"What are you doing here, then?" Bannerman demanded.

"Looking for you," Tom said simply.

"Why?"

Tom shifted the gun. "Because you set Wiley to ambush me. Don't tell me he had brains enough to act on his own! He was laying for me in the bush, but I got the drop on him. . . . Are you going to use that thing, or do you just carry it for coyotes?"

Once more Bannerman's glance went to the cabin. "I didn't set Wiley on you. If he's dead, he had it coming. He went crazy when Ruth threw him over. I sent him out to the ranch. Evidently he didn't go."

"Evidently," Tom said.

Into the rancher's face came a dry hardness. He told Tom angrily, "I take no responsibility for Wiley's acts. If he had anything to do with the shooting of Cincinnatus, that's no reflection on me. But if Ruth is in that cabin, I'll know who's responsible for *that!*''

After a moment, Tom chuckled. ''You know, you came close. Last night I asked Ruth to marry me. I told her she was of age now, and the hell with you.''

Bannerman's eyes were hungry for this. They gripped Tom's. ''What did she say?''

''She said, 'one dose of that kind of medicine was enough.' If I were you, and really wanted to find her, do you know where I'd look? At Agency siding. If she isn't home, and she isn't here, my guess is she's taking off again.''

''Why—why would she do that?''

''Maybe she's had enough of your strutting. Maybe she'd like to feel that she's got free rein to choose whatever man she wants, and do what she wants.''

He jammed his carbine into the scabbard.

Bannerman's face acquired its lofty arrogance. ''You don't have to talk big,'' he said, ''just because you've got Snaketrack. . . . Enjoy that land while you've got it. It may not be for long.''

Tom rode back down the meadow.

After a minute he heard Bannerman riding back up the saddle. A deep sense of peace was in him. Let Bannerman find out about Snaketrack when it happened. But even when the rancher went back on the land, he could not rob Tom of one victory—the victory he had won just now. Over a man named Carmody.

Tom met Ridge on the trail. ''Bannerman wasn't in this,'' he told him, ''Wiley was lone-wolfing it. But Ruth's at my cabin, and somebody's got to get her started over to Agency siding.''

''Maybe she won't go, Tom, if she was really waiting for you!''

Tom laughed. ''She'll go. She heard everything that went on between her dad and me. She wouldn't want a man who wouldn't stand up to her old man for her. She'll look for bigger game—maybe town marshals.''

Ridge grinned. ''Cut it out, Tom.''

SNAKETRACK

If she can just bake a green-apple pie, Tom thought, riding away, something might come of it!

It was late afternoon when he reached Soledad. The town appeared quiet. Perhaps it always looked quiet, he reflected, to a man at peace with himself. And even though he had lost Snaketrack he could not care so deeply as he had before. He had ten sections. A man could call that a start, rather than a finish.

As he approached the hotel, a small man in a black shortcoat and round-crowned Stetson came from the dining room. It was Lopez-Montezuma. The general walked to a bay stallion tied to the sagging hitch-rail. He laid a hand on its withers and spoke to it before toeing his boot into the stirrup. Tom recalled that he had always ridden horses that most men would consider half-bronc. He went up, turned the pony, and saw Tom.

For a moment they looked at each other. Tom saw the preoccupation of his face quickly give way to recognition, and in surprise he saw him smile. Lopez-Montezuma put his right hand out, the hand that never wore a glove.

"Tardes, y adios!" he said.

On guard, Tom watched him. "Goodbye?" he repeated. "Has that lawyer of mine sold me out already?"

"That lawyer of yours!" said the general, sighing and shaking his head. "I tried to get his promise to join my staff. A man like that wins battles before they are fought."

Tom had the feeling that anything he said might spoil what the judge had set up. And as though the Mexican saw his position and was sorry for him, he chuckled.

"Well, it was a good foray, but he matched me. I did not lie to you, amigo. I said you owed me twenty-eight thousand dollars, which was what you got for the pesos you received from my paymaster."

It opened up, then, and Tom felt an ease go through him. "But I got pesos, not dollars, didn't I? And what happened to the peso after Lopez-Montezuma was beaten?"

The general turned his palm over as if to let chaff fall from it. "Your country did the compliment of cutting its value in half. Evidently Washington thought I would make a better president than Diaz. When I was beaten—no,

when I lost that last battle, for you see I am not beaten—
the peso fell. Your judge asked questions until he found it
out.''

Tom could hear the judge explaining it to the Mexican.
That it was pesos, not dollars, his client owed, and you
could buy two pesos for what one would have bought
before. So that there was enough money in Tom's bank
account to pay him off, with a little left besides. . . .

Lopez-Montezuma was gripping his hand, all rancor
gone from his face. ''I leave you a poor man, my friend—
but what man is poor who owns land? In my country,
where only three or four own land, we know what poverty
is. Come back some day, and you may see twenty ranches
where today there is one. . . .''

When he rode away, he took an alley, cutting swiftly
down it toward the back lots leading to the river.

Tom felt the gladness coming up in his breast. It was
too strong for him to contain, and he jogged quickly to the
bank building and ran up the steps to the Cincinnatus
rooms. Laura let him into the parlor, her coolness ineffec-
tual against the gusto he brought. She put her finger on her
lips.

''Dad's asleep, Tom—'' Then, after a long, relieved
look at him she turned away. ''We've worried about you
all day. Why did everyone leave town so fast? What
happened out there?''

Tom told her about Morgan Wiley, and she stood before
the fire with no evidence of emotion. The room was
duskily illuminated by the ruddy surge of the firelight.
''Was Bannerman there?'' she asked at last.

''He was at my cabin, looking for Ruth. She was there,
Laura. Still thinking it could work, or just wanting to hurt
her father. I don't know. I caught him in the meadow,
before he went in.''

She turned quickly. He saw the shine of tears in her
eyes. ''You couldn't have planned it better, could you?
You were able to tell him about Ruth yourself. A man
wanting revenge couldn't have asked for anything better.''

Slowly Tom shook his head. ''I was able not to,'' he
said.

For a time she regarded him without expression, and then she reached her hands toward him. "Oh, Tom! I knew you could, if—if you'd let yourself."

"I decided a notch in a gun wasn't enough to take back to that goat pasture of mine," Tom told her. "I had to win out over somebody, though, and it turned out to be me."

"But you're not losing Snaketrack, Tom," Laura said gladly.

She was a clean, slender silhouette against the fire, and Tom went to her. He said, "I know. I met the general in the street. Where's Tig?" he asked.

"He's already left. He signed the lease and caught the train two hours ago. So it's just waiting for you."

Tall, tired and smiling, he held her there. "I may be wrong about your marshal," he said, "but I think he'd get over it if he lost out. Have I a chance, Papoose?"

"I told you I hadn't heen spoken for," she said.

Tom touched the soft braids of her hair, and said: "You're doing it the way I like it. A little bit Papoose, a little bit Laura."

"Chignon," she smiled. "It was in a magazine."

"Pigtails," he said. "Just grown-up pigtails." And he pulled her suddenly close. He heard her say his name in a soft voice, "Tom!" a whisper and yet a cry, and then she was still, and they stood close together in the firelight.

CLASSIC ADVENTURES FROM THE DAYS OF THE OLD WEST FROM AMERICA'S AUTHENTIC STORYTELLERS

NORMAN A. FOX

DEAD END TRAIL	70298-3/$2.75US/$3.75Can
NIGHT PASSAGE	70295-9/$2.75US/$3.75Can
RECKONING AT RIMBOW	70297-5/$2.75US/$3.75Can
TALL MAN RIDING	70294-0/$2.75US/$3.75Can
STRANGER FROM ARIZONA	70296-7/$2.75US/$3.75Can
THE TREMBLING HILLS	70299-1/$2.75US/$3.75 Can

LAURAN PAINE

SKYE	70186-3/$2.75US/$3.75Can
THE MARSHAL	70187-1/$2.50US/$3.50Can
THE HOMESTEADERS	70185-5/$2.75US/$3.75Can

T.V. OLSEN

BREAK THE YOUNG LAND	75290-5/$2.75US/$3.75Can
KENO	75292-1/$2.75US/$3.95Can
THE MAN FROM NOWHERE	75293-X/$2.75US/$3.75Can